A KNIFE
IN THE DARK

COREY MCCULLOUGH

A KNIFE IN THE DARK
2nd Paperback Edition
Copyright © 2018 by Corey McCullough

ISBN: 9780996690256

First edition published as THE NIGHT ALSO RISES © 2014 by C.B. McCullough
First printed in the United States of America in 2014

10 9 8 7 6 5 4 3 2

For
Robin Hart
Joanne Hart
Bill McCullough
Mary Lee McCullough

1

The music in the elevator is an old jazz standard played on clarinet. It sounds like it was recorded inside a tin can. When gravity stops trying to push me into my shoes, the doors roll open. I tug on my necktie, but it's as tight as it will go.

I step out trailing rainwater from my coat and hat, leaving wet footprints in the carpet. The foyer is something. It's like the front of a countryside mansion yet somehow still looks right at home here, 300 stories above the streets of Amber City. The only element I find unforgivably garish are the wooden double doors. They belong on a castle, not in a skyscraper. Emblazoned across the wood in gold is the word *Harland*.

The doors swing open, splitting *Harland* between the *r* and the *l*. Out steps a straight-backed little man with white hair, dressed in a perfectly pressed tuxedo with peaked lapels.

"Mr. Tarelli, I presume," says the little man. His voice echoing through the hall sounds like an opera singer.

"That's me," I say. My voice echoes, too, but more like rusted gears than an opera.

He takes my coat and hat with a professional flourish. "Mr. Harland is expecting you in the observatory," he says.

"I didn't catch your name," I say.

"Hennessy, sir."

"You smoke, Hennessy?"

"No. Right this way, sir."

Following Hennessy over the threshold, I find myself in the kind of place I've only ever seen in old films. It's a massive main hall with overhanging balconies, black marble floors, and accents of onyx. The doorways are flanked by larger than life white busts of figures from mythology and religion. My face is probably priceless as Hennessy leads me to a wide center stairway with ornately carved banisters. The hallway at the top has carpet the color of blood, and I pass beneath the painted gazes of a dozen giant portraits of men and women I feel like I should know.

Hennessy opens another set of doors leading into a very dark room. He steps to the side. He does not go in.

"Just through here, Mr. Tarelli," Hennessy prods.

I reach up to tip my hat, forgetting that he's holding it. When my hand touches bald scalp, I tug on my earlobe and nod to him as I enter. The doors shut behind me with a boom.

I stand still for a second, letting my eyes adjust to the darkness. The room is every bit as big as the grand hall but lacks any of the classical style. No pomp here. The only furnishings are a small dining table and chairs. The far wall is transparent— a single giant window, with Amber City laid out before and below like a sprawling, moving picture, blurred by the buckets of rain snaking over the glass. The sun has just gone down, and black clouds hang over the skyline, sparking with silent, horizontal lightning.

"I trust you found the place all right?" squeaks a voice.

The skeletal framework of a balcony runs along the midsection of the window-wall, connected to the floor by a switchbacking ramp. At the center of the balcony, a man sits in a chair.

"Hard to miss," I say.

The man gestures toward the dining table. "Please, help yourself."

On the table, I find one bottle, one glass, and a wooden box of long cigars. I only sniff the cigars, but I pour myself a drink and take a sip. It's got that uncommon aftertaste I've come to associate with good, expensive scotch. I drain the glass in a few sweet gulps, then refill it, thus aborting yet another honest attempt to quit drinking. Can't blame me. It's not every day a guy gets a free sip from the top shelf. And it's not every day a guy gets called on to visit with Rutherford Harland in person, either. Yet here I am, a stranger invited into his personal home—just hours after the murder of his only son.

One last try at tightening my tie, and I approach the

window-wall. I ascend the ramp with footfalls that clank and ring through the room. For the life of me, I don't know how someone could stand to live in a place that echoes so much. Then I'm at the top. With him.

Some colorless hair still clings for dear life to the back of his head, and a thin mustache droops from his upper lip. He'd be taller than me, standing, but it's been a long time since he's done that. Slumped in the metal frame of a wheelchair, a woolen blanket over his lap, Rutherford Harland casts an unassuming figure for one of the most powerful men on the planet.

He turns his gaze away from the city to study me with brown, red-rimmed eyes.

"Mr. Tarelli," he says. "A pleasure."

"Likewise, Mr. Harland," I say. "Beautiful place you've got here."

"I'm glad you think so. Rarely do I get the chance to entertain guests. . . . Isn't the view marvelous?"

"It's very lovely."

It's more than that. Not even from an airship viewport have I ever seen Amber City quite like this. Through the haze of rain, the city is rolled out before me like a living map. The skyscrapers are radiant towers. The streets are rivers of flowing light, and the headlamps of gridlocked airships hovering along in their exact, geometric paths high above the streets create spider-webbing, synthetic constellations.

"Dreadful night," Harland says. "Is the rain very cold?"

"A little. Nothing a stiff drink can't cure."

"I despise the rain," Harland says. "I was born and raised on Jannix, and I was almost middle-aged by the time I had the means to do any real traveling. It wasn't until then that I realized there are places in the star system where it doesn't constantly rain. It's not normal. Had I learned that at a younger age, I may never have stayed here."

"When you're right, you're right," I say. "It does rain too

much."

He makes a noise in his throat. I can feel myself squirming, and I hope he doesn't notice.

"About your son, Mr. Harland," I say. "For what it's worth, I'd like to offer my condolences."

Harland turns back to stare out into the night again, hands folded in his lap. "Thank you," he says. After what feels like a long time, he says, "How old are you, Jack? Sixty?"

"Fifty-eight," I say, "but who's counting?"

"Who's counting, indeed. Everyone who has ever lived has died, and yet we all still think ourselves immortal. We always think *we* are the exception. These days, every time that sun sets, I can't help but wonder if I'll ever see it again."

I slurp down the last of my drink, lean against the railing, and look out at the city. It feels like I'm hanging over a precipice. The last of the brown dwarf sun's light has faded away completely, leaving a black canvas dotted with a billion pinpricks of white light. Harland's not alone in his anxieties. Night falls hard on Jannix. With a synodic day of sixteen standard days, night lasts one hundred and forty-five hours here. We go almost an entire week without sunlight. It's enough to make any man wonder if he'll see another dawn.

"Help yourself to another glass," Harland says.

"I'd better not."

"Come now. You're young."

A little chuckle escapes my lips. "Been a long time since anyone called me young."

"All a matter of perspective, Jack. Take my son, one moment the pride of the Harland family name, on the cusp of inheriting my empire. The next, dead on some factory floor in East Amber. . . . You know why I asked you here tonight."

My lips are dry, and I wish I'd left something in my glass to wet them. "You want me to find out who killed your son."

Harland's reflection against the window is like the face that looks back at you from a puddle in the street. His hands aren't folded in his lap anymore. They're clutching the arms of his wheelchair like talons. His knobby knuckles are white.

I clear my throat. "With all due respect, Mr. Harland, we've never even met. I don't know how comfortable I'd be taking a client I don't—"

"You know who I am, and I've done my homework on you. That'll be enough."

"Maybe. But you don't know my methods."

"Jack, I have a personal security force *on call*. And I could hire every private investigator in this city if it pleased me. I need you because I have reason to believe the mob was involved in my son's death. They've been trying to take me down for years. To get at Nathan like this, it's possible they've infiltrated my business. Nobody associated with my companies can be trusted. And as for the police." He laughs. "They're even worse."

After swallowing, I manage, "Not all cops are like that."

"Enough of them are. I need somebody who won't cave under pressure. Somebody who's gone up against the mob before."

I feel my nostrils flare. "You know about that, huh? Well, then you know I lost."

"And I know you've taken too many falls to be a man easily bought. We're kindred spirits, you and I."

"Those days are long gone, but if you need a good private eye, I can give you some names. Guys who are smarter than me. Smoother, too. Me, I've got a temper. I strong-arm too much. Sometimes I drink too much, too."

"And sometimes you're too honest. In my book, that's the perfect man for finding the truth."

My teeth are grinding. I wish I weren't such a glutton for punishment.

"I work alone," I hear myself say.

"You will," responds Harland. "And you'll be compensated handsomely."

"I never doubted that." I look him in the eye, and I sigh. "You're a tough one to read, you know that? You must be good at cards."

"Dreadful," says Harland, without cracking a smile. "Too headstrong to bluff."

He extends a bony, long-fingered hand my direction. I grip it gently, and we shake. His skin is cold and soft.

2

Hennessy is there to meet me outside of the observatory. As the door swings shut behind me, I catch one last glimpse of Rutherford Harland on his balcony, looking out at the city. I'm still in shock over what I've just gotten myself into—a bum like me, suddenly under the employ of a man who probably makes more money in a day than I've seen in my entire life.

"My coat and hat?" I ask, because Hennessy's hands are empty.

"Mrs. Reed would like a word."

"Mrs. who?"

"Mrs. Reed."

"I meant, who is she?"

"Mr. Harland's daughter. She awaits you in the library."

"There wouldn't happen to be any more of that scotch in the library?"

"I shall arrange it, Sir. If you'll follow me."

As Hennessy leads me up an adjoining staircase and beneath more portrait-gazes, I'm trying to remember current affairs. This all happened so quickly, I didn't have much time in the way of research. I know from the papers that Rutherford has a daughter; a regular face at charity benefits and high society functions. Beyond that, I don't know much about her. Never thought I'd need to.

I can't help but wonder how Rutherford Harland even found me. In ten years as a private detective, I've never advertised once. Word-of-mouth business, exclusively. Mostly small cases; just enough to eat and keep the lights on. The murder of a business magnate like Nathan Harland—son of a legendary industrialist like Rutherford Harland, whose reputation approaches mythology. . . . This kind of thing isn't exactly in my wheelhouse. It's been a long time since I worked a murder case, let alone anything of this magnitude.

Hennessy leads me to another high-ceilinged room with the doors wide open. There are big windows here, too, but the curtains are all drawn. Every wall is packed to the ceiling with shelves upon shelves of leather-bound books—about as many books as a man could hope to read in a lifetime. Crystal chandeliers hang from the ceiling, and the walls glow from panels of recessed lighting.

Standing atop a brass stepladder on rollers, licking her finger to flip through the pages of a book, is a dark-haired woman, mid-thirties, with lean calves peeking out from beneath a long skirt.

Behind me, Hennessy announces, "Mr. Jack Tarelli to see you, Mrs. Reed."

"Of course," she says. "Leave us."

"Very good, Madame. And how do you take your scotch, Sir?"

"In a glass," I answer. "No ice."

As Hennessy hustles off in that straight-backed march of his, Mrs. Reed starts down the ladder.

"Your family seems to like high places," I say. I reach up to remove my hat, find it missing again, and instead just scratch my head. "I'm afraid I didn't know your drink, Miss. . . ?"

"*Mrs.* Reed," she says. "But Yvonne will do. Hennessy knows my drink. My, you are a brute of a man, Mr. Tarelli."

She's got a singer's voice: pleasant and husky. In a move that surprises me, she hops off the ladder still three rungs up, and her heels clack against the hardwood floor as she sticks the landing on sure feet. Her blouse is open at the top, showing her collarbones. Eyes like her father's, yet somehow entirely different. Fair skin. Red lips, upturned in a sly grin. Expensive makeup—a little much, for my tastes, but a lot of men like that. Her dark hair rests on her shoulders, and I wonder what it feels like.

"He's very lifelike," I say.

Her grin doesn't falter, but I can tell it catches her off guard. "What do you mean?"

"Hennessy. Practically human in every way."

She tilts her head a little. "What gave him away?"

"Well, he's not much for small-talk," I say, and I leave it at that.

It's true he's no conversationalist, but what really gave Hennessy away were his eyes. No matter how nearly perfect the simulation—skin, hair, vocal nuances, personality traits—you can always tell a bot by the eyes. They can be made to look quite real. Even the algorithm that controls their blinking is flawless, attuned to biological standards and automatically adjusting to conditions like light and humidity. The same goes for pupil dilation. What gives it all away is eye *contact*.

Eye contact is just too natural in humans to be successfully simulated in bots. It's controlled by situational cues, prior individual experience, anxiety, awkwardness.... The sorts of things machines don't have or feel. And unlike us, their peripheral vision is perfect. They don't need to look directly at something to see it clearly, as a biological eye does. Poor emulation causes bots to either roam the room with their eyes, seemingly at random, or never break eye contact at all.

"As you can imagine, it's difficult for my father to trust hired help," says Yvonne Reed, placing special disdain on the word, *hired*. "Bots are more trustworthy. One hundred percent loyal."

"A knife is loyal, too," I say. "But you can still cut yourself with one."

With perfectly rhythmic footfalls, Hennessy re-enters the library with a silver platter, carrying a short tumbler for me and a tall, skinny glass of something for brown-eyes, packed with ice. He stops before us and offers the platter without a word. Yvonne takes her drink, and I take mine. Hennessy stares straight at me, but his eyes seem empty, like he's seeing through me.

Hennessy turns to Yvonne. "Will there be anything else, Madame?"

"Not right now," she says.

Hennessy bows and exits with the empty platter tucked under his arm, and as the bot's footfalls fade away down the hall, Yvonne Reed and I touch glasses and drink.

"Is it just you three, then?" I ask. "Living in this big place?"

Yvonne sighs, and her eyes take a tour of the library. "It's a rather dreary old haunt these days, isn't it? Once upon a time, it was full of life and laughter. People were in and out all the time—visiting with my father, conducting business, you know.... These days, he's too old and paranoid for socializing."

"Maybe he's got it right. Look at what happened to your brother." Seeing the look on her face, I stop and clear my throat. "My condolences."

"Mentioned Nathan, did he?"

"He hardly needed to. It's all over the news." My glass is empty all of a sudden, so I set it down on a nearby end table. "Were you two close?"

"No, not very. Nathan is—or *was*, rather—nearly as old as my biological mother was. We had the same father but little else in common. Do you know very much about my father?"

"Oh, the usual. Self-made man. Climbed the ladder from the factory floor to the executive's office. Started his own company and never looked back. Hands in all manner of business across Jannix. Owns a stockyard on the Invictus moon, if memory serves. Occasionally married. Two children. Am I going too fast for you, Mrs. Reed?"

She tilts her frame to one side, cocking her head slightly to look at me. "Why so interested in my family, Mr. Tarelli?"

"Well, I'm not, if I'm being honest."

"Oh?"

"It's called small talk, Mrs. Reed. It's what you do while you're waiting for the other person to work up the courage to come out with whatever it is they really want to say. You're the one who called me in here. It wasn't just for a nightcap, was it? If it was, my glass is empty, so I'll bid you a fond farewell. I'm too busy a man to stand around jawing like this."

One of her dark eyebrows rises in an appraising sort of way. "I'm not accustomed to being spoken to like that."

"I'm sure you aren't."

"You can't blame a girl for being curious," she says. "Nathan's dead, and Father suddenly starts taking houseguests? Just wondering what's so special about you, is all."

"You let me know if you figure it out. Say, if we're gonna go round in circles like this all night, would you mind at least putting on some music?"

"I won't keep you, Mr. Tarelli. I mean well by my inquisition. I feel a certain responsibility to watch over my father in his old age. And all the more, now that Nathan is gone."

"Is that why a married woman your age is still living with her father?"

Her jaw tightens, and her eyes smolder. Her skirt spins in a wide arc as she turns away. With slow, measured grace, she walks back the way she came.

"Please thank your father for the drinks," I call after her.

She says nothing.

Hennessy's waiting for me in the hall, this time with my coat and hat.

3

I'm thinking about the intricate, spider-webbing constellations of airship traffic visible from Rutherford

Harland's observatory and wondering where I am, right now, in that marvelous view. And I wonder if at this very moment those brown, red-rimmed eyes are watching me.

The cab driver is cursing the congested boulevards of the skies in a sharp foreign tongue. Based on his accent and the twanging, quick-stepping music he's got playing in here, I'd say he's fresh off the boat from the Ul'ru Colonies up north. I'm in the back seat, thumbing through a wad of cash every bit as handsome as Rutherford Harland promised, and thinking.

Despite Harland's distrust of cops, he must still have some sort of pull within the Amber City PD. He's made arrangements for me to visit the scene of the crime: 105th Street in East Amber. But before that, I've decided to make a quick stop of my own. It's little early to stray off the beaten path, I know. But I like to do things my way.

Detective work is, after all, in my blood. Dad worked Amber PD Homicide Division, just like his father before him. I made it there, too—after a slight detour. When I enlisted with the Jannix Interstellar Navy at seventeen, it was mostly out of wanderlust. I knew what awaited me here. I had seen it in my father's face every morning, when I was just getting out of bed and he was just dragging himself home from work.

I wanted to spend a couple of years seeing the star system before settling down into that life. Given my family history and Dad's good standing in the department, I knew there would be a job waiting for me when I came home. Things might have even gone the way I planned, if not for the insurrections on Antioch. A year after I enlisted, I was called up into the Democratic Trade Coalition's Allied Military Forces and sent half a solar system away as a part of the initiative to ensure interplanetary peace—which, it turned out, meant making war.

I made a name for myself in battle. When I demonstrated a knack for tactics, I was made a combat controller. A few years passed, and I was made an officer. And a few years passed after that. Funny, how time goes by.

I saw a lot of death in that war. Caused a fair share of it, too. Too many good men are still buried in those gray sands.

The war went on long enough for a few more promotions. The enemy was never really defeated, but eventually, the worst of the fighting stopped. I came home to Jannix a retired Second Lieutenant. By then, Dad had passed away, but I still wanted to make him proud. I joined the Amber PD. My war-hero status and family legacy got me a spot in the Homicide Division, and I quickly made detective.

One of the first things you learn working homicide is that time is the enemy. The first twenty-four hours after a murder are a precious, precious thing. The trail goes cold along with the body. You've got to use wisely what little time you have. You learn how to survive on nothing but black coffee, bad sandwiches, and a little booze to take the edge off. Even in the war, I never understood what had made my dad such a bitter, hateful old drunk. But the nice thing about war: the blood and brutality serve a purpose. When you see it firsthand in battle, well, you can sigh and regret the war and lament what terrible things it pushes humans to do.

Homicide, though. That's a different story. When you see travesties and perversions committed on an hourly basis, amid the day-to-day existence of this city, where there is no war, no possible justification. . . . Well, the human condition is what you lament. And you start to hate the kind of world where people do these things to one another.

There are many reasons I wish Dad had still been alive when I made detective. But mostly, it's because only after I started doing his job, started seeing the things he used to see. . . . Only then was I finally able to understand my father as a person. As a man. All too late.

It's like Rutherford Harland said. All a matter of perspective.

I sit in the back seat of the taxi cab, watching the lights of the city fly by. Two years from sixty is too old for the average

Joe to still be doing this kind of work, especially alone. But I'm not your average Joe. I have no family. I have few friends. I have only one thing: a case, from a long time ago, that still needs solving. A case for which I must be prepared—in mind and muscle.

I work these private jobs to stay sharp. I spend my free time honing my body. I burn up my money on nutrition, supplements, and genetic enhancements to stave off the effects of age and keep me strong. Because when the day finally comes, I can't afford to be too old or too weak to get the job done. I live hell-bent toward a singular purpose. One that I understand on a certain level will probably never be fulfilled.

It's a bad life I'm living. But it's mine, and it's now, and it's all I got left.

The cabbie's jubilant, foreign-tongued exclamation snaps me back to reality. The traffic is clearing up.

With a hum of antigravity engines, the taxi hovers along, slipping down beneath the city lights visible from Rutherford Harland's observatory, and into the shadows they cast.

4

"Anyone ever tell you that you drink too much, Tarelli?"

"Just once. He drank his meals after that."

The bearded twenty-something kid across the table laughs.

The Neon Monkey is clouded with smoke tinted blue and swirling in visible currents. Onstage, the house band is deep into a mellow set.

He goes by the name of Fox, and he's young enough to be my son. He's covered in tattoos and dresses like a gang member, but that's just an act. In reality, he's one of the best-connected brokers of information in all of Amber City.

I've placed his customary fee on the table: a drink to open his mouth, and a couple hundred credits to get him to say something worthwhile.

"I don't buy it," says Fox. "Nobody *sees* Rutherford

Harland."

"I did," I say.

"Old man must be getting senile."

"He probably is, a little."

"I was talking about you."

I reach across the table to take back my money, but Fox is quicker, snatching the bills up between his fingers and rolling them into a little, paper tube. I lower my hand and close it into a fist on the tabletop. He takes a drink.

"Rutherford Harland?" says Fox. "We talking about the same guy? The shipping industrialist? The richest man in Amber? One of the richest on the planet? Ten billion in property values within the city limits alone? Net worth—?"

"The same one," I cut in. "And the same one whose son was found dead on a factory floor a few hours ago. What do you know about that?"

Fox cocks an eyebrow. "You got some angle here, Jack?"

"You've got this backward. I pay *you* to talk."

Fox smiles. "I might have something juicy."

"Go on and impress me."

"Nathan Harland's always been high up in his dad's companies, but in recent years, he's kind of kept his distance from the old man, working mostly off-planet. Whether for business reasons or something personal, I don't know. But then, all of a sudden, Nathan moves back home to Jannix and starts living with Rutherford at his mansion—until recently." He punctuates this thought with an impious slashing motion across his throat and a lolling of the tongue.

"You're practically reciting his obit," I say. "Give me something I can use."

I'm bluffing. I didn't know Nathan had been living at home with Rutherford and Yvonne. If I had, the first place I'd have gone would have been whatever room he'd been staying in. If Rutherford just forgot to mention this fact, that's okay. But if he intentionally left it out, lied by omission, then I'm going to have a problem.

Fox takes another drink, swishes it around in his mouth, savors it, takes his sweet time just to get on my nerves. I wonder if he realizes most working folks don't sit in bars all day and night.

"Here's the thing," says Fox. "A large sum of money changed hands on Invictus about a month ago in exchange for several blocks of the condemned factory district in East Amber. At the time, it piqued the interest of some of my clients, so I did some digging. What's funny about it is, no record of the transaction exists. So I get my hands on the documents, and guess what I find? The buildings are still all listed as condemned. They belonged to the City of Amber until recently. But now, they belong to somebody named Royal Evening."

"And no bill of sale?"

"None. One day the records say one thing, the next something else."

"Royal Evening. Some sort of corporation?"

"It's listed as an individual."

"Sounds like a front."

"That's what I thought. So I dig some more, and I find a possible match: a decommissioned starship by the same name. The *Royal Evening* was a luxury spaceliner that was retired and melted down for scrap about fifteen years ago. And the owner of the *Evening*? Surprise, surprise. Nathan Harland."

"Hmm."

"Like I said, bank records indicated that some big money changed hands on Invictus around that same time the properties came under new ownership. There's no data trail to connect the two, but you do the math."

"And Nathan Harland also happened to be working on Invictus at the time, didn't he?" I say. "The property purchase could explain why he moved home. There was a new investment he had to keep an eye on."

"You haven't even heard the kicker," says Fox. "Ready for this? The properties in question: twenty-five square blocks worth of real estate, located between 99th and 106st in East Amber."

East Amber. 105th Street. The factory where Nathan Harland was found dead.

I flag down a waitress, pay for my drinks, and tip her. I stand from the table and adjust my hat. "I'll be in touch, Fox."

Fox chuckles. Guys and gals in his vocation have no names or numbers to keep in touch with. They exist only in the back sections of bars like the Neon Monkey, and only when they want to.

5

Fox's information is not all news to me. I had inklings of some of it, but I see now that the connections are even more black and white than I suspected. I also knew the scene of the crime was a factory, but I didn't know it was a condemned one. That raises even more questions as I hail a cab and tell the driver to head to 105th.

Perhaps visiting the scene of the crime conjures images of dusting for fingerprint, scanning for biological material, or taking blood samples to run DNA database queries. If only things were still so simple.

There was once any number of means to scientifically divine the identity of a suspect. When the Coalition's systemwide citizen database contained the full DNA profile of every human being born in a hospital for the past 300 years, solving a crime was as easy as finding a hair or a flake of skin.

If human DNA wasn't present in a homicide investigation, there were other options. You could scan for cross-transfers of bacteria and match the bacteria's DNA instead. Or match a strand of virus found on the victim with antibodies to that virus present in the perp's bloodstream. I've read cases of murders that occurred in closed rooms, where chemical compounds secreted from the killer's sweat glands hung in the air long enough to be collected, and the amino acids in the proteins were reverse-translated into DNA.

If you had dandruff and B.O., a life of crime was an ill-advised career choice.

It all sounds very exciting, which is why the myths of super-science crime fighting are still perpetuated in popular culture. Police in the movies are always in lab coats, working over fancy equipment late into the night, trying to discern a bit of DNA or mRNA or a grab-bag of other acronyms. In reality, white-gloved investigating is a thing of the past.

You could write a book about the downfall of science in criminal investigations. Someone probably has. I haven't read it, but I have a feeling it would start something like this. Once upon a time, criminal investigation was like math; you swept the scene for biological evidence, narrowed it down according to the timeframe when the crime was committed, plugged the results into a database, one and one is two, there's your man.

But at some point (about thirty or forty years ago), a trend emerged in medical research—a transition from mechanical and cybernetic prosthetics for amputees, to lab-grown, fully grafted biological replacements. The method was already well established in the growth of internal organs, but using the same techniques to grow flawless new skin, muscle, limbs, digits, and eyes was revolutionary. But every output needs an input, and the process often involved borrowing organic matter from one or several donors.

Over time, crime scenes started to become a bit more complicated. It wasn't uncommon to find the DNA of five or six people at a crime scene, all present within the time frame of a murder. Cops thought they were dealing with multiple perpetrators and were led around in circles, tracking down—and occasionally roughing up—false leads who would turn out to be donors of the genetic material used for some scumbag's lab-grown teeth or something.

The first major outcry came from a news story that broke about an ongoing police manhunt. The suspect had been at large for over six months. His DNA and fingerprints had been found in the middle of a nasty murder scene. Something like 2 million credits of taxpayer money had been spent on the investigation before a simple public records search revealed that the suspect thought to be "at large" had been dead for ten years. Turned out, he had donated his body to public health, and his biological material had hung in deep freeze in a genetics lab for a decade after he died. Said material was subsequently used to grow a new hand for a guy who's lost his in a work-related accident—and then used his shiny new hand to kill a neighbor who'd been sleeping with his wife.

Later, it was determined that the real killer's work-related "accident" had been a calculated act. This guy had altered his insurance plan to specify biological limb replacements *only*—in the event that such a procedure should ever become necessary—even though it would cost him a bundle extra. Then, a month later, he fed his own hand to an industrial metalworking planer. All this to plant false evidence at the scene of a premeditated murder. It was innovative, you got to give him that.

This man had a clear motive, opportunity, and no alibi. Yet he managed to get away with murder, overlooked by investigators who were too busy feeding data into computers to use their heads. The guy was gone and totally off the grid by the time the police realized their mistake. He was never caught.

A prime example from that era is the "Rug Ruse," when an elderly man with no past arrests, no history of violence, a back problem, and a heart condition, was convicted and sentenced to death for the brutal slaying of four teenagers during an apparent drug deal gone wrong. The evidence against the old man was a DNA match to a handful of hair found in one of the dead boys' hands, clearly torn from the killer's head. But the whole thing was turned upside down when an investigative journalist, of all people, uncovered the truth.

The story goes that the barber of the convicted old man also happened to offer genetic hair "restoration" as one of the more upscale services in his shop. His business partner, his son, was a researcher in medical genetics at the University of Blacksparrow Technical Institute. Their hair restoration therapy made them a little money on the side, and there was nothing technically illegal about what they were doing. For years, their source material came from one cheap, seemingly harmless, and basically endless supply. Each time the barber finished a cut, he simply cleaned out his comb over a basket in the corner. At the end of the week, the basket would be full of hair—not *cut* hair, but hair he had combed from the heads of his clientele. Hairs shed during combing commonly had the roots still attached, and hair follicles are a rich source of biological material . . . including DNA.

Unfortunately, the poor old man who got the book thrown at him for quadruple homicide never knew any of this. His name wasn't cleared until it was too late. He died on death row while awaiting his fate, ruined and disgraced, never knowing that his hair was growing in the scalp of a killer—and a rather vain killer, at that. The historic, interplanetary headlines read: *SCIENCE OVER LOGIC! COURT POSTHUMOUSLY OVERTURNS DECISION AGAINST INNOCENT MAN DEAD AND DEFAMED BY 'RUG RUSE.'* It wasn't the first false conviction to be overturned under such circumstances, but it was the first time the issue was brought into the spotlight, igniting public ire and inciting a general loss of confidence in investigative police work.

Soon, organized crime dipped their ladles into the stew. Syndicates like the Blue Wreath started constructing false evidence for similar frame-ups, and suddenly all manner of suspicious crimes were being committed, peppered with biological evidence from suspects with no motive, sometimes not even opportunity. All this might lead one to believe that new laws and standards of practice would be mandated for the growth of biological material. But the limitless wealth of the medical and consumer genetics industry, plus increasing distrust and disdain for law enforcement, led the tide to turn the opposite direction. Against the police. The wrongful conviction scandals spearheaded rounds of harsh legislation against the use of DNA and other biological evidence in court cases, which became increasingly strict over the years. Nearly every form of biological material is no longer admissible in court. Even if it was, it would only make things more complicated; it's easier to fake DNA than to fake a cold.

While there is no legislation barring the use of DNA in police investigations, it is *very* illegal to bring a case against anyone based solely on genetic/biological material, to say nothing of simply being misguided. Old-school cops—specialists clinging to tradition—still use biological material to find leads, but these days, mild variants of genetic alteration and implantation are used in everything from beauty products to dental hygiene to fitness and body decoration—even pet care. Finding reliable biological evidence involves sifting through so much junk material that it's really more trouble than it's worth.

The result of all this was a great backward leap in the field of police investigation. A new breed of detective—really an old breed reborn—rose to the occasion. The modern investigator uses logic, deduction, and hard-nosed fieldwork to track down his man.

Reason. Motive. Hard physical evidence. Anything less is nothing. My grandfather worked in white gloves. But my father was part of that transitional generation. He relearned the old ways. Worked in street clothes. Wore down the soles of his shoes tracking leads. Bloodied his knuckles on anything that got in his way.

As for me, as my taxi hovers down to street level and I step out onto 105th, East Amber, I'm not wearing any white gloves.

And I'm sure as hell not here to dust for fingerprints.

6

Several Amber PD cruisers with lights off are parked outside the factory. The rain is pouring down, and I arrive just in time to see a big, white car with the words "Amber Morgue" on it lift off and hover into the night sky. They've loaded up the body and taken it away.

I quietly curse Fox and his drink—and myself. But Harland told me the cops had agreed to hold the body until I arrived. Must've gotten impatient. Now, I've missed my chance to see the body. Maybe they'll let me in at the morgue.

The approach of my tall, broad-shouldered frame, half-concealed by shadow and rain, has a few of the nearby officers getting nervous. I take my hands out of my coat pockets and let them hang at my sides. It always makes a cop feel better when he can see hands.

The nearest one, a little guy, adjusts his cap by the brim and clears his throat. "Help you?"

"Jack Tarelli," I say. "Rutherford Harland sent me down to have a look at the body."

His relief is almost comical. He extends his hand. "Wilmer O'Hara, Homicide," he says.

I shake his hand gently. Don't want to hurt the little guy.

"My partner Albright's the one you want," he says. "Go on in."

I pass Wilmer and his associates and walk through the open door of the factory's freight entrance. Inside, I'm given only a partial reprieve from the rain. The place is falling apart, with holes busted through the ceiling so big that the rainwater comes in like a trickle in some places and like a waterfall in others. Nearby, some of the standing water swirls down a storm drain. The rest sits in deep puddles. I try to pick my way through without getting too wet but end up splashing up to my ankles in a few places. Can't imagine a man of Nathan Harland's status ever thought he'd meet his maker in a place like this.

Lighting units have been set up to illuminate the scene, and a few cops are still snapping images. Center stage is a blood-spattered mess. No body, of course.

A big plainclothes cop stands nearby puffing on a cigarette. He's middle-aged, with a high and tight haircut speckled with gray. He's taken off his jacket, leaving his chest holster exposed. He looks sour already, but at my approach, he positively pickles.

"Press found us already?" the big guy growls. He's in charge. Got to be Albright. "Get this inbred out of here."

"Albright, I take it," I say. "I'm the PI Rutherford Harland sent down to look at the body." I take an exaggerated look at the bloodstained floor behind him where the body used to be. "Looks like we've got a second mystery on our hands."

"Rutherford wants his own man on the case, that's fine," Albright says, "but I can't wait around all night for some freelancer to come play detective."

"You were told to hold that body until Harland's man got a look at it," I say.

After one last drag, Albright tosses his cigarette over his shoulder. It lands in the water with a hiss. He makes no attempt to avoid the puddles as he closes the gap between us, never breaking eye contact with me. He's a big guy. Almost as big as me. Almost.

"This is not the night to test me," he says. "I know how you think this works. You act tough enough with us, and we'll bend, right? Cause that's what you do when a jealous husband pays you fifty creds to tail his wife down to a motel in a shady part of town. Well, nobody bends around here, pal. They only break. This is where real work happens. Real detectives. Real stakes. Turn around and go on home, and maybe I won't have my boys rough you up for disrupting a police investigation. Got that? Old man?"

The bored sort of way he says it, like he's giving directions to a lost motorist, gives me no doubt he isn't bluffing. And I remember how we used to do things. Boy, do I. But instead of backing off, I step forward, closer, slowly, and look down at him. We'd be nose to nose if he were a couple inches taller. I widen my shoulders, flex my traps so my coat lifts up, making me look even bigger. Then I lower my voice to a rumble.

"If you or your boys take a run at this old man, you're liable to take that body's place. You got *that*? Junior?"

Albright doesn't retreat, to his credit. He just stares up at me. Out of the corner of my eye, I see the other cops watching us.

Finally, Albright grins. Chuckles. He steps past me—not backward, which is important—and takes out a pack of cigarettes. He lights up another one. Puffs casually.

"Jean-Luc Albright," he says, sighing out smoke and rubbing his temples. "Whatever you're going to do, get it over with so we can all get the hell out of here."

"Jack Tarelli," I say. "May I?"

He waves a dismissive hand toward the floor. I take the cue and kneel down to take a look.

This part of the floor is higher ground; unlike most of the factory, it's relatively dry. Congealed blood coats the concrete nearly half an inch thick in some places. Thinner streaks run out along the perimeter. There's no sign of footprints in the blood, which strikes me as strange.

"Any leads on who called in the tip?" I ask.

"Who told you about that?" asks Albright.

"You, just now," I say.

Albright actually chuckles again. "Ass," he says. "Yes, it was an anonymous tip. Caller said Nathan Harland would be found dead at this address."

"Ten to one odds the caller was the killer," I say.

"No way to know yet," Albright says. "Body probably wouldn't have been found for a long time, otherwise. Nobody around here but bums and junkies. The whole district is a ghost town. They should just blast it."

"Clear-cut murder?" I ask.

"Better believe it," he says. "Whoever did it wanted him to suffer. Shot six times. Both knees, both elbows, both eyes. I'm guessing in that order."

"That explains all the blood," I say. "Major arteries, plus shock value with the limbs. Then overkill with the eyes. A bad way to die."

"Overkill is right. Nearly blew the top of his head off."

"The top?" I take my hat off, scratch my bare head, a bit envious of Albright's gray-speckled dark hair. Nice and thick. Mine hasn't looked like that since I was twenty-five. "Any weapons recovered?"

"None. Harland wasn't armed, either. He must not have come expecting a fight."

"What makes you say that?" I ask.

"For one, he wasn't carrying so much as a pocketknife—"

"No. I mean what makes you think he came here? You're assuming he was here of his own will. Don't assume anything."

Albright bristles a little at that remark, probably he remembers who he's talking to. A PI. A gumshoe. A shamus. The lowest of the low, in the opinion of a commissioned detective. I know. I've been on both sides.

"Was he robbed?" I ask.

Albright grabs something from a nearby cop and hands it to me. It's an evidence bag. I take it carefully, holding it up to the lights to look through its transparent skin. Inside is a gold watch with a crystal face—probably worth more than Albright's salary—and a bloodstained, leather wallet.

"Anything in the wallet?" I ask, knowing better than to try looking for myself. That would ruin my welcome real fast.

"ID, about a thousand credits in bills, some bank cards, and a couple datachips worth who knows how much."

I hand the bag back to Albright. A lot of money in there. Even if the motive wasn't financial, who wouldn't take this stuff? Was the killer too worked up at the time to be thinking clearly? Or somebody who doesn't need money?

"You got pictures of the body?" I ask.

"No can do," says Albright.

"I don't want to take them anywhere, just to have a look."

Albright growls in annoyance. It looks like his cigarette's about to split between his teeth. "Then you're gone," he says.

"Then I'm gone."

He gestures to one of the nearby officers, who is quick to comply. He brings over a datapad, which he keeps firmly in his grasp, but he allows me to look at each picture for a moment as he scrolls through.

I see various angles of the somewhat portly body of Nathan Harland lying face-up on the factory floor with dark, ragged wounds. Due to the gunshot wounds to his knees and elbows, his lower legs and forearms lie at strange angles. His mouth hangs open a little like he's watching a bad movie, but where his eyes should be are only two coin-sized holes. I can see no other noticeable injuries except for some discoloration around his neck.

The officer scrolls past another picture, but I reach up and quickly scroll back—Nathan Harland from the neck up.

"Albright," I say. "The exits on the head. Near the top of the cranium?"

"Yeah."

"Looks like almost a forty-five-degree angle, upward."

"The coroner will tell us," Albright says. He takes the datapad away and nods to the other officers. "Let's pack up, boys."

I give the crime scene a final glance and turn to leave, but Albright grabs the shoulder of my coat. I turn back around.

"I do not want to see you again tonight," he says.

"Feeling's mutual," I say.

"I mean it. Stay out of our way, or there'll be trouble."

"Let me give you some friendly advice."

"What?"

I lean in close, so that only he can hear me. "Get your hand off me, or I will break your damn fingers. All of them."

He tightens his grip. "Then I'll arrest you for assaulting an officer."

"With broken fingers, you will."

Albright lets go. I leave.

7

Exiting the factory, I pull up my collar and adjust my hat against the cold rain. I weave through the cops standing guard, leaving them and their patrol cars behind and walking down the street. I'll hail a cab in a minute. Sometimes a walk in the rain does the mind good.

Even though I managed a peek at those pictures, I can't help but wonder how much more I could have learned from a firsthand look at the body. Albright wasn't just in a hurry; he clearly meant to send a message by having it taken away before I got there. To show he wasn't going to be pushed around. I'm just grateful I was able to learn as much as I did.

First impressions: Something strange is going on.

In any homicide investigation, you're generally dealing with one of, or some combination of, three options. Blades, firearms, and particle beam weapons.

Standard pistols, rifles, and shotgun firearms are the most common choice among Amber City killers. "Firearm" is a misnomer. Classic firearms used a spark and flammable powder to create a miniature explosion, propelling a projectile—like a metal bullet—down the length of a gun barrel. Modern firearms, however, use synthetic bullets launched by means of artificial acceleration. The same tech used in the antigravity boosters of automobiles and airships is used to accelerate a slug down the barrel. Rather than the potential energy contained in a shell full of powder, the energy processes are initiated by the weapon itself with a rechargeable power pack. The result is the same, but ballistics is now a science of physics, not chemistry. Antigrav-accelerated bullets are affectionately nicknamed "akslugs," and rather than the explosive bang produced by firearms of yore, the discharge of a power pack is like a whisper, making akslug weapons as quiet as they are deadly.

A smaller percentage of crimes involve particle beam weaponry. Particle beam weapons are deadlier than akslug firearms, but thanks to the higher price tag, fewer make it to the streets. Particle rifles and particle pistols emit charged particles in the form of a concentrated, short-burst beam. These blasts are capable of burning through flesh, bone, and nearly anything else. Where a bullet can rip, tear and destroy, a particle beam will burn and disintegrate matter in its path. They work best at medium range. Beyond that, the beam will bloom, spreading out and diffusing into a less harmful cone of light, then fading away altogether. While these weapons might seem unstoppable, the modern personal magnetic force field—a scaled-down version of the tech used by starship shields—was designed specifically to defend against particle beams. If properly calibrated, a personal force field covers a person's body like a second skin and can defend against a full power pack's worth of point-blank blasts from a particle pistol before needing to be recharged.

In this case, the lack of burns rules out particle beams; no need to scan for radiation. Nathan Harland's knees and elbows were all but destroyed, leading me to believe that the killer used either an akslug shotgun, or a handgun at very close range.

This was not a dispute that got hot or a stick-up gone wrong. Nathan Harland was killed with calculated, carefully chosen shots. Nathan Harland was not murdered. He was executed.

Content with my walk in the rain, I wave my hand over a nearby signal pylon. It illuminates with white light, and within seconds, a set of headlamps breaks off from the zigzagging traffic lanes high above to come whizzing down in my direction.

Typically, the next step in the investigation would be to case the neighborhood, ask a lot of questions, search around, that sort of thing. Like Albright said, there's no one around here but vagrants and drug addicts, but they can be valuable sources of information. Now's not the time, though, because four big men in trench coats have been following me since I left the factory. And they're getting closer.

I don't think they're cops, and I don't know what their game is, but I'm not sticking around to find out. Against one, maybe even two, I might try my luck. But four to one? Unfair odds for any man.

As the cab lowers to a hover beside me, I hazard a glance over my shoulder just in time to see them take a seemingly casual turn down an adjoining alley. I step into the cab and shut the door, and we take off.

"Take her down a couple blocks, then circle back," I tell the driver. "Nice and slow."

When we come back around, I press my nose against the glass, trying to see down into the street below. The signal pylon is dark; they didn't hail a cab to follow me. That's about as much precaution as I can take, so I give the driver an address a couple streets down from home, and he redirects the cab toward the other end of town for some much-needed sleep. I wish I was still young enough to pull all-nighters, but a guy needs his rest.

8

She's the first thing I think of when I wake up, and she's the first thing I see. She smiles at me from the photograph on the bedside table, illuminated by the dim, synthetic glow of the clock face. She wears a white dress.

I switch on the light and get out of bed. I have to do it right away. Otherwise, I'll just lie here thinking bad, bad thoughts. And on a planet where night lasts for days, you can't wait for the sun to come up. I have a hangover. Bought a bottle on the way home and drank the whole thing after I got back here last night. I was supposed to be quitting, but the stuff at Harland's was too good. It's always too good and never good enough, and all over again, I can't get enough of what I don't want.

Since moving into this two-room hovel nearly a decade ago, I've hardly changed a thing. Same flesh-colored walls. Same uniform carpeting. No decorations. The few additions I have added are a weightlifting bench and a comprehensive electronic workdesk. I go to the fridge in the corner and retrieve my breakfast: raw eggs and stimulant pills washed down with a couple glasses of water. Then on to the weightlifting bench. Not one of those fancy antigrav/ultragrav variable-resistance models. No, I prefer the old-fashioned kind. With big, damn heavy weights. Made of metal. Tech bothers me sometimes, And besides, there's something savagely divine about the act of man moving steel.

The jingle of metal weights kissing one another to each repetition is music to my ears. My chest burns with sweet agony as blood pumps into the muscles. The white-noise chorus of rainfall against my solitary window intensifies. I recall the words of Rutherford Harland. How he hates the rain. Most people do. I don't mind it. The only thing better is thunder.

An hour later, thunder shows up. It tolls like the strike of a gong. Sweat coats my ugly, hairless head. I put up the last rep of my last set and place the bar on the rack. For a moment, I sit on the bench, listening to the storm, breathing deeply, feeling my body pulse with every heartbeat. No man of my age should have to work so hard. But this is the life I have chosen. Devoted to a cause. When the day comes for me to fulfill my destiny, maybe I'll fail, but it won't be because I'm too weak, too slow, or too out of breath. All this will be worth it. All the lonely nights, all the bad thoughts, all the hard work. All good, and damn worth it.

An image flashes across my mind's eye: Maria's body, the

way I found it. The knife. . . .

I lie back down on the bench, grab the bar with my big hands and push it off the rack. I can do more. I can go harder.

Fifteen minutes later, sweat is running into my eyes. The vein in my forehead pulses with blood flow. My breath hisses through clenched teeth at the apex of every press. It feels like I'm killing myself.

With a last grunt of effort, I put up the final, final rep, and I lie there, panting like a dog. My shirt is stretched tight. I can see the bulge of veins through the fabric.

After my heartbeat slows back down to resting rate, I return to the kitchen to down a heavy-duty, genetics-based muscle growth supplement. It rushes through my bloodstream, fueling my cells like coal to a hungry furnace. I grab my datapad from the bedside table and dial Harland's number.

"Hello?" says a posh voice.

"That you, Hennessy?" I say, mopping my head with a towel.

"It is."

"Jack Tarelli here. I know it's early, but I was hoping to have a word with your boss."

"Mr. Harland is in his study and has asked not to be disturbed. May I relay a message?"

"It's a bit private. Just let him know I called, will you?"

"I believe Mrs. Reed would like to speak with you, sir."

"Mrs. Reed? I don't want to talk to her."

A pause.

"She insists, sir."

"I bet she does."

"Here she is, sir."

I start to protest, but it's too late.

"Mr. Tarelli," says Yvonne Reed. "What a pleasant surprise."

"You ever leave the house, Mrs. Reed?"

"Is that why you called?"

"Maybe. Now be a good girl and run and fetch Daddy, won't you?"

"My father is a very busy man. I'm afraid you don't understand how lucky you were to meet with him once. If you think he's going to drop everything for drinks whenever you have the inclination, you're in for a disappointment. His time is precious."

"You, on the other hand, seem to have more of it than you know what to do with."

"He is grieving over the loss of his son," says Yvonne. "And your visit seemed to upset him even more. I don't know what you said to put him in such a state, but frankly, I wouldn't mind if you just left him alone and never called again."

"Does Daddy Dearest know you screen his calls like this?"

"Only when I think such disturbances might affect his health."

"Oh, that's all right, Yvie. You seem disturbed enough for the both of you. I wonder—just why does it bother you so much not knowing what your father and I talked about last night? You think if you keep me on the phone talking nonsense long enough I'll let something slip?"

A short pause.

"I don't presume to understand all of my father's business," she says. "I only care about his well-being. If this interruption is essential, I can transfer you to his office."

"Thank you," I say.

She hangs up.

When I call back, to my surprise, Harland answers personally.

"Hello, Jack," he says.

"Mr. Harland. I apologize for calling you up like this, but before I get any deeper into all this, I was wondering if you might clear something up for me."

"Oh. I will if I can."

"Do you have any idea what your son was doing in that

abandoned factory?"

Harland goes quiet. I wait, patiently, like a good fisherman does. I want to know—without so many words—whether or not Rutherford is aware of those property purchases, the disappearing act of the title transfers, and/or his son's possible involvement in the patch of real estate where he was found dead.

After a few moments of dead air, Harland makes a thoughtful sort of noise in his throat. "Pardon me," he says. "Sometimes, it's hard just to think. I feel like my mind has gone dull, like an old blade. It's like a disability. The sharp, old luster is gone forever, and I know it. . . . You ask me what he was *doing* there. It implies that you believe he was there of his own volition."

"Just covering my bases. Keeping an open mind. Otherwise, you run the risk of seeing mirages in the desert, so to speak."

"A true professional. I'm afraid nothing comes to mind. If I'd suspected Nathan was doing anything that would put him in danger, I'd have kept a sharper eye. . . . What a strange and terrible thing to talk about him in the past tense like this. It isn't right. The blessing of living to old age is also its greatest curse: defying the natural order of things."

Harland clears his throat. I can't tell if he's grumbling in frustration or holding back tears or both.

"Check your bank account, Jack. Your fee has been deposited."

"Pardon me, sir, but you already paid me yesterday. Remember?"

"I remember," Harland snaps. "And now I'm paying you again."

I quickly scan through my datapad, accessing my account, and my jaw drops.

"This. . . . This must be a mistake, Mr. Harland. It's double what we agreed on."

"It is. But it's no mistake."

"I see. Pay double what's expected, expect double the results? Something like that?"

Harland makes a funny, humming sort of noise. "Such a relief to work with someone of intelligence for a change."

"I'll let you go, Mr. Harland."

"All the best to you, Jack. Keep your wits about you."

"Same."

9

The undying night can play tricks on your mind, but the traffic in the skies is a clear indication of midday as my cab flies over the industrial zones that ring the outskirts of Amber City like cancerous growths. The cab drops me off in the dirty little neighborhood known simply as Port Town: a noncommercial spaceport district home to various methods of interplanetary travel, legitimate and otherwise. Not my favorite place to visit. On the bright side, it's stopped raining for the moment.

I pay the driver and step out into the street, right into a large puddle. The water goes over my ankle, down into my shoe. I swear and hop on one foot as the cab takes off.

People are everywhere; assorted breeds of rogues and miscreants. It's an old understanding that the Amber PD leave Port Town alone. Despite its unsavory nature, this district brings in a lot of money. The legality of such matters is a technicality to which the city is willing to turn a blind eye for the sake of the almighty credit. The only law here is bouncers and hired muscle.

The streets are lined with bars, taverns, and ratholes advertising pleasures for sale. I shoulder past men and women of all sizes, shapes, and colors, wearing a patchwork of clothing and armor from across the star system. I see akslug pistols holstered at hips, particle rifles strapped to backs, and wicked blades sheathed on forearms and ankles.

A broad-shouldered, unnaturally muscular fellow wearing an all-black breather mask with two Xs scratched into the eyes of the visor goes out of his way to elbow me as we pass. I bounce off him. My blood boils, but I keep on walking.

It's been a long time, but the neon sign is still there, partially blown out and flickering. *Good Caesar's Garage*. For a moment I stand there, thinking of days gone by. Days when that sign wasn't blown-out or flickering. Back when I came here not as a shamus, but as an Amber City Detective. On a weekly basis, my partner and I would visit "Good" Caesar: the owner and operator of this establishment, and a snitch for the Blue Wreath mob. He'd feed us info, and we'd pretend not to notice the illicit activities going on in his chop shop. But that was over a decade ago—back when there was still the occasional police presence in Port Town. Back before Blue Wreath won.

I can hear the bug-zapper buzzing of the neon sign above me as I step through the doorway. A sensor catches my movement, and a two-note salute echoes through the building, announcing my arrival. The place looks more like a cave than a garage, with the skeletal remains of hovercars, small airships, half-disassembled bots, and other unfortunate machinery lying dejectedly throughout. The roof drips from the seam of a set of bay doors.

The big man at the counter barely looks at me as I approach.

"Need to speak with Caesar," I say.

"Ain't here," says the big man.

"Need me to say it again?" I say, louder this time.

That gets his attention.

The big man sneers. He wears a mechanic's jumpsuit with an out-of-place, skinny necktie. He outweighs me by a good seventy-five pounds, but it's mostly fat. He's got a face like a bulldog. One of his eyes wanders.

"Ain't here," he says again. "Get your ugly mug out of here before you regret it."

"People lose teeth over words like 'ugly.' Look. . . ." I lean forward and place my palms on the counter. "I'm not some goon here to work him over, no more than you're a mechanic.

I just need to talk with him a minute. Don't make me get physical. I'm an old man. You're apt to make me pull a muscle."

The big man leans forward too, mimicking my move, but with one small adjustment: He puts one hand under the counter where there's certainly a weapon. A sawed-off shotgun, if I were him.

"What makes you think I'm not a mechanic?" he demands.

He's only just finished the question when I grab his necktie and drop all my weight to the floor.

His face slamming against the countertop sounds like a bowling ball bounced off a sidewalk slab. Before he can react, I stand, wrap my arm around his head, and pull him the rest of the way over the counter—where he can't reach that weapon— and hold him suspended there.

"Mechanics don't wear neckties," I growl into his cauliflower ear. "Bound to get them caught in something and get churned up real nasty."

A stream of words in a foreign language erupts from the far end of the room. I turn to see a skinny little man standing near the rear doorway of the garage. He's dressed in a similar jumpsuit stained with grease. Thin, scruffy fuzz sprouts from his unshaven face, and his eyes stare at me with fright.

"Hey, Caesar," I say, still holding the struggling thug as blood dribbles from his nose. "You caught me in the middle of teaching some manners to your doorman—"

Caesar turns on his heels, flings open the door, and takes off into the darkness.

"Damned if you don't need a lesson, too." I pull my hostage headfirst over the counter and toss him to the floor. Before he can recover, I roll over the countertop. I dash through the back door just in time to see "Good" Caesar turn and race down a back alley.

I clench my hands into fists and pump my arms as I make chase. I turn the corner and barely manage to avoid a pair of trashcans toppled to slow me down. Picking my way around them, I knock a gawking bystander to the ground and keep running. I can see Caesar up ahead—

He turns around, aiming something at me. I throw myself to the ground, realizing a moment too late that it isn't a gun. He's fooled me. He throws the empty beer bottle at me, and it shatters a couple feet in front of me. When I look up, he's gone.

"Caesar!" I yell, getting to my feet.

I jog to where I last saw him. The rusty, metallic frame of a fire escape ladder is still trembling against its counterweight. I look up at the roof, growl a curse, and grab the rung of the ladder to begin my ascent. But a tiny rattling noise from behind gives me pause.

I look over my shoulder and see the boxy frame of a metal dumpster in the shadows. Panting from my run, I take a deep breath, stomp over to the dumpster, and throw open the lid.

Caesar is huddled inside. At his exposure, he tries to hide by pulling a garbage bag over himself. I reach in and grab a fistful of his shirt.

"Up you go," I say.

I haul him out and place him on his feet in the alley. No sooner have his shoes touched the pavement than he tries running again, only to be yanked back like a dog on a chain. I hold him by the shoulders in front of me, trying to lend him a bit of the dignity he can't seem to find himself.

"Don't kill me, Mr. Tarelli!" he sputters in thickly accented speech.

"*Kill* you?" I say, genuinely surprised. He looks up at me, sniveling. "I came here to talk to you, not to kill you."

He doesn't look convinced, so to show him I mean it, I let go of his shirt and stand with my palms open.

A yellow smile with a few missing teeth breaks across his face. He all but falls apart with relief. "Oh, Jack Tarelli!" he says, slapping me on the arm. "I see you breaking the nose of my associate, and gives me quite a scare. Today I did not want to be *crushed,* into pieces."

"Well, it's early, yet. Why'd you think I was here to kill you?"

Caesar waves it off. "I have policy. Too many people trying to kill me these days, and too hard to remember which ones. I decide, *run*. Then think. I am still alive, so it has worked so far. Let us talk in shop."

Caesar gestures for me to follow him, swatting clinging garbage from his hair and jumpsuit without pretense.

The big doorman is waiting for us. Blood wreathes his nose, lips, and jaw. In his hands—as I suspected—is a sawed-off akslug shotgun. Before he can use it, Caesar rattles off some speech in his primary language. The thug shoots me a walleyed glare, then unhappily tucks the weapon back under the counter.

As we walk by, I take the handkerchief from my breast pocket and toss it to the thug. "Your nose is running."

He growls. The handkerchief falls to the floor.

10

"You almost gave me a heart attack, Jack! Never thought I'd see *you* again."

Sitting at a small table in the back room of Good Caesar's Garage, I've positioned my chair facing the door. Not that I think a saint like Caesar would try anything funny. But you can't be too careful in Port Town.

"When you stopped coming around my shop, stopped asking questions," says Caesar, "I think I am about to be shut down. But then, I heard of your arrest." Caesar's face stretches out into a stinking smile. "You were in prison all this time?"

"I never went to prison," I respond flatly. "The charges were dropped."

"You know what the news called you? Jack *the Knife*, the Six-Shooter—"

I hardly even realize I'm doing it. One moment, I'm sitting there, trying to keep my cool. The next, the table we're sitting at is in two. It falls in splintered pieces to the floor, sending up a cloud of dust. My fist hovers in mid-air where I smashed through it.

Caesar sits on the ground, having tilted his chair backward in terror and tumbled to the floor. One of his hands is raised in feeble defense, shaking.

It's a chore to open my fist. I stretch out my fingers. Flimsy table.

"I don't like that name," I say.

Caesar's throat bobs from a hard swallow, and he nods once.

"Look," I sigh. "I'm here on a case."

"A case? An investigation, you mean?" Caesar gives the halves of the table a nervous look, then tentatively rises to his feet. He rights his chair and sits back down. "You are still police?"

"Private eye."

The grin on Caesar's face is now smug and knowing. It doesn't take a genius to know what he's thinking: How the mighty have fallen. I try to ignore it.

"So, how about it?" I say. "For old time's sake, we do a little business?"

"What could I have that you want?"

"Information. On the Blue Wreath."

Caesar's grin dies.

"Your investigation involves the mob?"

"That's what I'm trying to figure out."

"No," he says. "I *cannot* help with that."

"You can. It's whether or not you will."

"I don't talk to *anyone* about that anymore. Blue Wreath is too big. Too powerful. Too dangerous to leak information."

I know better than most what he means about the danger. It wasn't exactly safe back when I was a cop, either, but it was never this bad. Prior to the war on Antioch, there had been several major crime syndicates on Jannix, each with claims to delineated territories. In big cities like Amber, it was particularly bad but manageable. But then, when Jannix's best and brightest went off to fight the war, one of those syndicates got ambitious. Started annexing neighboring territories, branching out into all kinds of new activities.

The Blue Wreath Boys—named for the Blue Wreath nebula visible in the southern sky of Pirol once every ten years—became so large and powerful that they absorbed almost all competitors, becoming a worldwide force of organized crime on Jannix. Nowadays, their influence extends all the way across the star system, including Pirol. The word "mob" has practically become synonymous with the Blue Wreath.

By the time I traded in my army uniform for a badge, the Blue Wreath was the number one enemy of Jannix law enforcement. Amber City was their hometown, and for some cops, like me, mob activity was of the highest priority. My partner and I specialized in homicide cases with suspected links to the Blue Wreath, and there were plenty of them.

At that time, Good Caesar was running his chop shop with mob backing, and for a little grease money, he passed along information to us. Information that helped track down quite a few killers.

But that was almost fifteen years ago. A lot has changed. For everyone.

Nowadays, the Blue Wreath owns Amber City. That's not a matter of debate. It's theirs. They've got a stake in almost every facet of business and industry.

A shaky, unspoken truce now exists between the police and the mob. Every so often, one side will send a message just to show they still mean business, but justice isn't being done in this city anymore. Crime runs rampant and unchecked. Some say it's a necessary evil. I say it's rotten. Not surprising that Harland wanted to find somebody outside the police department to investigate his son's murder.

It's funny to be sitting with Caesar like this, so many years later. Like two old war vets swapping stories about the bad old days. The days before Jack the Knife.

"Royal Evening," I say.

"What?" says Caesar.

"*Royal Evening.* Does the name mean anything to you?"

Caesar shrugs.

"What about the name Nathan Harland?"

Caesar's eyes bulge a bit. He lowers his voice to a whisper. "Is that why you have come here? You think *I* know what happened to him? And you think Blue Wreath was involved?"

"Nice of you to ask all the questions for me."

"I don't know anything."

"Sounds like you know he was murdered. And you must know what a thorn Rutherford Harland has been in Blue Wreath's side. He's never caved to the mob. And he's proud of it. Killing his only son would send a pretty clear message to the old man, don't you think?"

"I'm telling you, Jack, I don't know—!"

"I absolutely believe you," I say, standing up. "And I'm not here to try to beat anything out of you. That's not how I conduct business. But I do know how, if the mood strikes."

I reach into my pocket—causing Caesar to flinch—and pull out a wad of cash. I peel off a few hundred-credit bills. I hold them out to him.

"Consider it a down payment," I say as his grease-stained hand nervously accepts the bills. Then I fish around my jacket pocket and come out with a half-credit coin. I flip it in his direction, and he catches it against his chest.

"What's this for?" he says.

I gesture to the pieces of the table on the floor. "Piece of junk couldn't have been worth more than that. Keep in touch, Caesar. Double-cross me, and I will be back. *That's* when you'd better run."

I don't wait for an answer. I leave the back room and see my own way out, keeping a close eye on Caesar's thug. He shoots me another glare but nothing more. I notice he's taken off his tie.

11

"'Jack the Knife.' That's what the media started calling him. 'The Six-Shooter Killer.' As unforgiving, deadly, and cold as a blade. And how cold. How cold a man would have to be, to do something like this to a fellow human being. How cold . . . to do it to his own wife."

It's twelve years in the past, and the district attorney's voice has the measured and practiced tone of a stage actor. He turns from the jury. He presses a button. A picture appears onscreen. The air in the courtroom grows thinner, sucked down by a collective inhale of shock and disgust.

Another push of the button, and the image is replaced by a new one. Disgust turns into despair. The DA keeps quiet, letting the pictures do the talking.

I try not to look. Even after seeing those pictures a hundred times, having hard-copy prints waved in my face, seeing black-boxed, edited versions flash across the news, and seeing the real-life, unedited versions plastered to the backs of my eyelids there to meet me with every blink. . . . Even after all that, it hurts. Hurts just as much as the very first time I saw her lying there.

Sitting at a table in the front of the courtroom, I turn away because I know which picture comes next. The jury does, too. They've seen them all a dozen times or more throughout the course of this trial. But familiarity does nothing to soften the blow for them, either. In a way, it only makes it worse. Knowing what's coming has them curling their lips in anticipation, flinching preemptively, like a dog about to get smacked. There's fear and regret in their eyes, but there is something else: a morbid fascination. Why? Because here is something truly irredeemable, justifiably despised. And over the course of two and a half months, about nine Jannix nights, the prosecution has been chipping away at a barrier, blurring the line between the crime and the defendant. Shifting the hatred for the act, and redirecting it onto the individual. Placing Jack Tarelli in the line of fire.

And the scary part is, it's working.

The DA flips to the last picture. Somewhere in the courtroom, a woman cries out. Grown men turn their heads.

I hold no animosity toward the people of the jury. They can only react to what they are shown. It's the prosecution who's to blame. It's not enough that I lost my wife. It's not enough that my life has been ruined. They just keep pouring salt into the wound. They just keep twisting . . . the knife.

"I'd like to return, for a moment, to the issue of the weapon," says the DA.

Of course he would. The lack of evidence against me has his team rehashing the same old stuff.

"No weapon was recovered from the scene of the crime," says the DA. "As stated, the Blacksparrow City Ballistics Lab determined the weapon in question to have been a powder-based firearm, possibly a large-caliber revolver. Laymen will know this better as the celebrated 'six-shooter' of untamed frontier days. Today, I have brought with me a similar model for the benefit of the jury's deliberation."

I sit up a little straighter. This is new.

With an air of prestidigitation, Mr. District Attorney retrieves his attaché case from the prosecutor's table, opens it, and draws out a weapon: a giant, chrome-plated revolver.

Distress ripples through the courtroom at sight of the weapon, with its long, thick barrel and heavy-duty, skeletal frame. It's almost a foot long from hammer to nose, and it takes two hands just for the DA to hold it. His fingers are wrapped tightly around the carved, wooden handle.

"A Grantz-Stillitz Double-Action Model 9," he says. He flips open the swing-out cylinder for a view of the large, empty chambers within. "Holds six rounds, and fires a 50-caliber bullet via smokeless powder. I've never seen one fired, myself, but I'm told that when discharged in darkness, this weapon can turn night into day. A single blast can cause temporary hearing loss."

He sits the six-shooter down on the table with a gut-shaking thud.

"A powder-based firearm is an uncommon choice of weapon," the DA says, massaging his wrist. "Less than 3 percent of violent crimes committed since the incorporation of the city of Jannix involved powder weapons, and because they are not well-matched to the needs of military or law enforcement, consumer demand is low. Grantz-Stillitz is one of the few specialty manufacturers still making powder-based weaponry products. Those they sell go mostly to collectors and sport shooters."

I find myself barely listening. My eyes are instead locked on the giant chrome revolver on the table. All I can hear is what I imagine the blast of that gun must sound like: thunder on earth, exploding in my head. Over and over. Over and over. And over and over again.

Six shots.

"The bizarre choice of weapon calls into question the killer's motives," the DA is saying. "Some sort of calling card, maybe? Or a sick, twisted joke? Jack, here, is no stranger to firearms. On the night Maria Tarelli was murdered, Detective Tarelli was carrying standard issue Amber PD weaponry: a 38-caliber accelerated slug sidearm. He is certified in its use and has discharged it several times in the line of duty. As an infantryman in the war, Jack would have become quite familiar with the popular 30-caliber 'Sandblaster' carbine. He would have also been highly trained in the use of fully automatic particle beam assault rifles and other varieties of weapons with which soldiers of the day were expected to be proficient. In addition, investigation of the premises of Detective Tarelli revealed a small arsenal of personally owned firearms—from handguns to shotguns and one particle rifle. Jack claims these were all purchased legally for home defense and *sport shooting*.

I will concede to the defense that no 50-caliber revolver was found to be in Jack Tarelli's possession, nor among his collection. Nor are there any records that Jack did, at any time, legally purchase a powder-based firearm of any kind. However. His collection tells us a lot about him."

The district attorney waves a disgusted hand at the table and continues, "No petty criminal is carrying one of *these* things. A weapon like this is, arguably, only of interest to a gun enthusiast. A collector. And as for the defense's claim to the murder being a possible hit, somehow linked to local organized crime. . . . First off, I ask you: To what end? And second: What is a lowlife, scum-of-the-world hitman for the mob doing with a weapon like this—a valuable collector's item that is practically an antique?"

The district attorney turns to lock eyes with me. Or at least it will appear that way to the jury. The truth is, even he can't look me in the eye for what he's doing to me. Instead, his gaze is firmly planted at the top of my head, where a little bit of hair yet remains. It'll be gone soon.

"This wasn't mob violence," he says. "It was an isolated incident, committed by a paranoid and overworked individual who has spent so long on the front lines, here and abroad, that he's become desensitized to death. A husband who thought he could get away with murder by using an unregistered weapon from his personal collection because, as an officer of the law familiar with criminal investigations, he knew it would be practically untraceable. He *did* this thing, ladies and gentlemen. Jack Tarelli is Jack the Knife. He is the Six-Shooter Killer."

12

Nathan Harland.

Shot six times.

I throw the scotch back and let it trickle down my throat. I savor the burn. I bathe in its numbing, healing aura.

I sit alone, in a corner booth of the watering hole not far

from my apartment. Nobody bothers me as I work, scanning my datapad through the news articles that have been run since the murder of Nathan Harland. I've lost track of how many drinks. I shake my head, trying to clear the haze. Trying to clear it of memories of the courtroom, the pictures, the six-shooter on the table. . . . And the connections. The six shots that killed Nathan Harland have me playing connect-the-dots. And as for the possible link to the Blue Wreath. . . .

I try to take another drink, but my glass is empty. My hand is shaking.

I bang my glass against the table.

"No ice!" I growl.

The bartender's a skinny wisp of a thing, and he hurries to comply; doesn't bother trying to get the empty glass from me, just fills up a fresh one. He knows me—knows I have a temper sometimes. Not two weeks ago, I left some upstart's teeth on the floor for getting too familiar. I should quit drinking.

Maria Tarelli. Just one unsolved case in a city full of them— a case that's over a decade old, now, and should just be let go.

But I haven't let it go.

I feel the muscles tightening beneath my sleeves. A hairline fracture cracks in the empty glass in my hand.

"Damn right, I haven't."

The wispy bartender brings my drink, sits it on the table, and leaves quietly. I flip my datapad to the next article.

NATHAN HARLAND MEMORIAL SERVICES
ANNOUNCED

Deceased's father, billionaire Rutherford Harland, to receive guests in Amber City's Botanical Gardens, in his first public appearance in almost twenty years. . . .

I've read this all already, and thus far have been rewarded no great insight, but rereading the same information in slightly different wording has at least helped me to digest and familiarize myself with the family history of the the Harlands: the legendary, self-made billionaire Rutherford, the quiet, number-crunching son Nathan, and the spotlight-loving philanthropist daughter Yvonne Harland Reed.

> Amber City Detectives declined to provide details regarding the cause of death, but one officer commented, "The pallets in that factory looked like they had not been moved in years. It would have been a long time before anyone found the body if we hadn't been directed to it by an anonymous tip."

I stop.

I reread the final paragraph twice more, just to be sure of what I'm seeing.

I briefly consider trying to contact Detective Albright right here and now, but decide against it, sauced as I am. Better to head home, sleep it off for a few hours, then get hold of him. I shouldn't have come here in the first place, but Caesar's unsolicited reminder of the past rattled me up something good.

I shut my datapad off and put it away. I finish my drink and drop a crumpled wad of bills on the table. I stand—

And the world goes lop-sided.

I brace myself against the table, double-clutch, and start again, this time more carefully. I tip my hat to the bartender and cross the gently swirling room, past patrons who pay me no mind. My drunkard's gait is practiced, hardy, and capable.

I notice, just a little too late, the occupants of the table beside the door: four big, silent men in trench coats, each of them staring at me so hard you'd think I was a naked woman walking on her hands. I exit through the front door as casually as possible. As soon as the door swings shut behind me, I duck low and slip left. It's raining again, damn it.

The tilting world plays tricks on my footing, and I nearly fall twice as I race through the rain, toward the corner of the alley that leads home. I draw the 44-cal akslug pistol from my chest holster as I run.

"Should have been paying closer attention," I scold myself. "Scratch that. Should have just had a water."

I practically crawl the last bit of the way, and I've just made it around the corner when I hear the bar door swing open violently and crack on its hinges against the outside wall.

I crouch behind a garbage can for cover. The world is rotating around me. I shake my head, trying to put it right, but no dice. I'm three sheets to the wind and in no condition to hold my own against anybody, let alone four men who presumably are in the business of holding *their* own.

Not in a fair fight, anyway.

I pull the flash grenade from my jacket pocket, remove the pin, and let it cook. I hear the hurried smack-smacking of shoes against puddles, coming my way. The countdown runs in my head:

Five, four, three, two–

I throw my weight into the garbage can. It falls over and spills across the street. The flash grenade blends in with the rest of the trash.

I turn my back and hear the electric pop-whine as the grenade discharges. For a split-second, the alley lights up bright as the sun. I hear a chorus of surprised screams.

Still ducked low, I swing around the corner to take inventory of my pursuers. Of the big, trench-coated men, all four are holding pistols. Three are on their knees, stunned and temporarily blinded by the flash. But the fourth—who either anticipated the attack or is just lucky enough to have avoided direct eye contact—is still standing. His face lights up nastily as he sees me. He swings his pistol and fires.

There's an eruption of brick and mortar as the accelerated slug blows a hole the size of a champagne cork in the wall beside me, erasing any doubt of what these men are here to do to me. Whatever happens next, remember they had it coming.

I squeeze the trigger and pop him three times in the chest, fast. The zip-whirring reports of my akslug rounds sound like hummingbirds. He goes down. I advance, nearly fall over, and crack the nearest of the stunned killers with the snout of my pistol, just above the bridge of his nose. His eyes roll back, and he sprawls over, unconscious.

One of the remaining men aims toward the sound of my footfalls and fires blindly in my direction. I hear the strange, sucking sound of the bullet's trajectory as it whizzes by, inches from my earlobe.

I react out of pure reflex; it's less a dive for cover than a semi-controlled, drunken fall as I hit the ground, taking cover behind the other remaining thug. I hear two more reports, followed by painful shouts as thug number one caps thug number two in his blind firing. The poor sap tries to tell his buddy to stop, just before he's hammered twice in the chest and goes down. It's just sad. No guy wants his death to be funny.

I roll and see the blind-firing thug taking aim again at the sounds of my movement. Lying sideways on the ground, I'm holding my pistol with both hands, praying for dear life that despite the way the world spins around me my aim is true. I squeeze the trigger.

ZIP.

The thug's head jerks backward. He looks angry at his own rotten luck as he turns slightly, fires once into the air, and smacks dead against the street.

I waste no time. Scrambling through puddles, I hurry to remove the gun from the hand of the thug I knocked cold. I pat him down for additional weapons—

The sound of footsteps. I wheel around, raising my pistol— at the bartender, aiming a shotgun at me. I don't drop my gun, but I do put my hands up. The bartender takes the hint and lowers the shotgun.

"You hurt?" he asks.

"Call the police," I pant. "Tell them to send Detective Albright. Mention the Nathan Harland case."

He turns to hustle back into the bar.

I bind the hands of the unconscious thug behind his back using my necktie. The other three are dead. I try not to bloody my hands as I check their pockets. Nothing but a few personal items. No ID, of course.

It takes my body a while to believe the danger's passed. I breathe a shaky sigh of relief and sit down, leaning against the wall, feeling the rainwater soak through my trousers. The wail of approaching sirens drifts down through the rooftops. "Got to quit drinking," I say to no one.

13

I run a hand over my bald head. In all the excitement, I don't know where my hat went.

The alley is bathed in the on-and-off-and-on-again flashing of reds and blues. The lone survivor among my attackers is currently being loaded into the back of an ambulance. He gives me one last deadly look before the cops shut the door behind him.

In front of me, Jean-Luc Albright is standing there, turning my pistol back and forth in his hand to examine it.

"Your mother ever tell you not to play with guns?" I say.

"You got a permit for this?" he asks.

"In my other suit."

"And this?" says Jean-Luc, using his datapad's stylus to hold up the clamshell-like remnants of the discharged flash grenade.

"Oh, they don't make permits for that," I say.

Albright doesn't laugh. His little partner, Wilmer O'Hara standing beside him looks even less amused.

"He reeks," O'Hara says to Albright.

"You're no petunia yourself, Wilmer," I say.

"I mean you smell like you're drunk," Wilmer says. "Give

me one reason why we shouldn't arrest you right now."

"Am I only allowed one?"

"Now listen, Jack—" Albright growls.

"No, you listen," I growl back, standing to full height. Both of them flinch. "They started the trouble. I finished it. I just took four killers off the streets—off your streets." I let out a disgusted breath. "And you wanna arrest me. Should be pinning a medal on me."

"So you confess to killing them?" Wilmer says.

"I was attacked without provocation, I responded out of fear for my own safety and the safety of civilians around me, and deadly force became necessary."

This one actually draws a smile from Jean-Luc. I've just recited—nearly verbatim—the Civilian's Right to Self Defense, as defined in the Democratic Trade Coalition's interplanetary code of law.

Behind us, the ambulance with its lone survivor lifts from the ground and flies away with lights bobbing back and forth lazily. Albright watches it go, then tosses the flash grenade shell in a rainbow arc, directly into the open lid of a nearby dumpster.

"You get anything out of the guy?" he asks.

I shrug. "Nothing good. We exchanged words when he came to, but he didn't feel like chatting."

O'Hara speaks up. "What does this have to do with the Harland case?"

"What d'you mean?" I say.

"The guy on the phone said—"

"Did he?" I say.

O'Hara's cheeks go red. I shouldn't have done that. Should have at least let him finish his sentence, but I'm still pretty sauced, and it's got my tongue looser than it should be. O'Hara starts to say something, but Albright touches his shoulder and gestures toward the bodies in the street. He takes the hint and trudges off.

Albright turns back to face me. He lights a cigarette, scratches his five o'clock shadow. "I'd lecture you about disrupting police investigations, but I guess you already got a pretty good idea what I'd have to say, Detective Tarelli."

"You read my file, huh?"

"I knew I'd heard that name before, so I looked into it. I remember your trial. I was pretty green at the time—working a beat down in Titan City. . . . For what it's worth, I thought you got a raw deal. A lot of us did."

He pauses here. I don't say anything.

"It's bad, what's happened to this town," says Albright. "These days, you can't tell what side anyone's on."

I stare him down. "Yeah. Never can tell."

Albright sighs out a cloud of smoke. Hands me my gun.

"If you happen to see my hat—" I start to tell him.

"Don't push it," he snaps. "You got us down here. Might as well tell me what you want."

"I want to know the condition of the body of Nathan Harland."

He's genuinely befuddled for a second. "You saw the photos."

"I mean the condition on arrival. Before you moved the pallets."

I watch the befuddlement morph into understanding, then a sort of appraisal. "How'd you know about that?"

"A reporter for the *Daily* printed something one of your boys said. Something about the body never being found if not for the call, because the pallets looked like they hadn't been moved in years. Thing is, I was there. Not only were there no pallets near the body, but I didn't notice any sort of discoloration on the floor. If there had been pallets sitting there in the same place for years, you'd be able to tell. So something was moved. But it didn't look like your boys moved anything to me."

Albright hesitates, then makes up his mind. "Well, they did, but you're right."

"Come again?"

He sighs. "The caller gave us an address and said we'd find Nathan Harland in the abandoned factory, buried under some equipment. When we got there, we found a bunch of rusty old pallets, big metal ones, stacked up right in the middle of the factory floor."

"So you move the pallets, and you find the body. Right where the caller said it would be?"

"Right. But it took some work. Harland had been . . . entombed under the things. And like you said, no discoloration on the floor when we moved them. They'd been piled up. Recently."

"Somebody was trying to hide the body," I say. "Kind of ruins my theory about the tipster being the killer. Why go through all that trouble to hide it if you're just gonna call the cops?"

O'Hara is waving for Albright to come over. He's in the middle of a call on his datapad. Maybe something related to the case.

Albright unceremoniously flicks the cigarette butt at the dead bodies behind him. "You'll be called in for questioning about this, Tarelli," he says.

"That's fine," I say. "Just not tonight. I have work to do."

"You mean you don't like to have your work interrupted?" says Albright.

I grin. Message received.

Albright nods a grim-faced goodbye and heads over to join O'Hara, who relays some information to him that I wish I could hear. Then they walk to their cruiser and get in. An unexpected feeling creeps up and blindsides me. Envy. A homesick sort of feeling for my old job, for the life that's so far behind me.

The cruiser hovers off the ground and starts to ascend, but then it lowers back down again. The door opens. Albright leans out.

"Tarelli," he shouts over the whine of antigravity engines. "You were right. About forty-five-degree angles."

He shuts the door again. The hovercar lifts, turns, and takes off into the night sky at terrific speed.

Officers are cleaning things up and taking photos amid flashing cruiser lights, but nobody seems bothered as I search the garbage strewn across the street. I manage to find my hat. Somebody's stepped on it, though, smashing it all out of shape, so I leave it there.

I circle around the bar, heading not for home but the opposite direction. My close brush with death has me jumping at shadows, and the words I exchanged with my attacker when he woke up—words I chose not to disclose to Albright—have me even more on edge. Every dark alley hides a killer, and every sound is a hitman tailing me.

Twenty minutes later, satisfied I'm not being followed and sick of walking in wet pants, I cut back along the side streets for home.

14

Once upon a time, I could take a punch and move on. Nowadays, I can still take a punch all right; it's the moving on that's tough.

Pain isn't just pain anymore. My nerves fire differently. It's like they get stuck in a loop, don't know when to stop. But far worse, I simply can't recover the way I used to. It's not about toughness or willpower or even taking the right drugs. My body's susceptible to injury, no matter what I do. And when I do get hurt, it takes a long time to heal. One careless mistake, one wrong step, one little fall, can change everything—which is a problem in this line of work, where a limp or a twisted ankle could mean the difference between getting home for dinner and getting zipped up in a body bag.

I barely broke a sweat in that shootout outside the bar, yet my knees feel like they've been lubricated with acid. I lock the door behind me and trudge into my apartment, shedding my wet clothes. I grab a tin of painkilling salve and sit down on the bed. I apply a glob to my knees and start massaging it in. The salve has a distinct aroma that I associate with my father.

I lay back on the bed, gritting my teeth. The pain is only getting worse. It'll come back down, in a minute or two, but for now, I'm a man who wants to fight trapped in a body that can't. It's a grim reminder that I can work out all I like, get strong, stay fit, take all the right supplements . . . but it doesn't change the places inside me worn down from long years of hard use. I hate feeling this way. Old. Vulnerable. Brittle.

I wasn't always so frail. Once during the war, I had a gunshot wound go untreated for six hours without getting laid up. We'd taken a desert command post by night, and in the chaos, I somehow managed to take a slug to the hip, which became something of a problem when an enemy convoy, returning from patrol, peaked the horizon. They caught wind of trouble right away and opened fire on us.

Our medic, as luck would have it, was the first to go—taken out by a rocket along with all his supplies. Our only chance was to hunker down in the Virofs' own trenches and hope they didn't charge. So there we were: dead of night, pinned down, outnumbered at least twenty to one. The skies were too rough for assault ships or troop shuttles, so no reinforcements. I called in an orbital strike. But these things take time. Satellite targeting, relayed to gunships in orbit that then need to calibrate for atmospheric conditions, then reposition themselves along the correct orbital path and wait for a clear shot.

For five hours, we were pinned down under heavy fire, exchanging shots with the convoy, trying to hold them back. Gray sand rained down on us in the trenches from bullets peppering above us.

Gunfire killed some of our guys. Mortars took others.

This one guy. Clancy, his name was. Or Chancy or Chaney or something. A sharpshooter. He was a machine. Killed at least four dozen Virofs that night. Just kept shooting and reloading, shooting and reloading. Finally, he says he's out of ammo but remembers a weapons cache fifty yards rear.

"Clancy," I tell him—or Chancy or Chaney or whatever. "Get down and stay down. Strike's incoming. 'Til then, you sit tight."

"No disrespect, Sarge," he says, "but nothin' doin'. We either keep shooting, or we sit and wait to die."

"You stay in this trench, soldier!" I shout at him. "That's an order!"

But he doesn't listen. He jumps up and takes off for the cache.

The guy made it about three steps before I heard the pop-pop-pop of slugs punching holes through his body armor—in through his back and out through the front. He probably never even knew he was shot.

It can't be more than a couple minutes after Clancy's shot down that my man on the horn gives me the word. "Strike is incoming. Take cover."

Take cover. Right. I ask him what he thinks think we've been doing for the past five hours, and he thankfully pretends not to hear me.

Somewhere in space high above the surface of Antioch, gunship cannons open fire, tearing clean through the atmosphere.

I'll never forget the sound. An orbital barrage—manmade, cobalt blue lightning strikes, supercharged beyond imagining—hitting the planet's surface like meteors, disintegrating anything in direct contact, detonating along the periphery, burning half-mile-wide craters into the desert, turning sand to glass.

Even after the Virof convoy has been erased from existence, it's still another hour before we can get a medic in to patch up my hip. Clancy's dead, along with half my unit, and I don't even take bed rest. I go out on patrol, as scheduled, the next day.

I dip my hand back into the salve and apply a generous portion of the analgesic to my right elbow, tender from hitting the street in my dive for cover.

Funny that I'd be thinking of Clancy on a night like tonight, twenty odd years since my last tour on Antioch. I used to think it was bravery that made him run for the cache that day. I've met a lot of guys like him over the year. Guys who never back down, never falter, never surrender. Guys who fight on, no matter what, without fear.

Until they run out of bullets.

As long as Clancy kept firing, he was master of his destiny. What would have saved his life that day was doing the one thing he couldn't do: sitting and waiting, and giving up control.

War is a series of charges and retreats. Those who never charge never win. But those who never retreat once in a while don't live long enough to win, either. Sometimes, you've got to know when to limp home and lick your wounds.

Lying on the bed, looking at the ceiling, I breathe deeply. The pain is pulling back a bit, and I'm pretty much sobered up. Now I'm just tired. Just going to rest my eyes. Just for a minute.

15

I dream I'm in the courtroom. Maria is there, but she's only a reflection in the blade of a giant knife. And in the background, men are ignited by an orbial strike turning a desert into an ocean of glass.

Hours have passed by the time I wake up. Much longer than I meant to rest. And another hour passes by the time I shower, dress, and take a cab into East Amber, back to the factory where Nathan was found.

I'm here, but my mind is stuck in that other case from long ago. Stuck in that same old spiral of thoughts. If only I'd come home that night when I said I would, maybe I'd have gotten there in time. Maybe I could have saved her.

And later, maybe if I'd listened to my gut—ignored the advice of counsel and set out after the killer in a manhunt of my own—I could have caught him myself, instead of sitting on trial for weeks, watching as my life was torn apart, my good name dragged through the mud. Watching as I became a scapegoat for both the public's disillusionment with law enforcement and the DA's outrage over unrest in Amber City.

As the cab leaves me standing on 105th Street, I rub my eyes, trying to push the thoughts away. The maybes and if-onlys will drive you crazy if you let them.

I was not found guilty, but I was not found not-guilty, either. Some legal technicality resulted in a mistrial, and rather than attempting to re-try me, the city dropped the charges. It was the right decision. There was no evidence against me, only opportunity and the age-old "jealous husband type" motive, which was shaky at best. The DA had seen what a slog it would be to get a conviction, and he was up for re-election that year. Another trial would have cost the city hundreds of thousands of credits and been a black mark on his record without a conviction, compared to the small smudge of letting me walk on a technicality. To the public who didn't know any better, the whole thing reeked of corruption.

Headline: CHARGES DROPPED AGAINST WIFE-KILLER COP JACK 'THE KNIFE' TARELLI, THE 'SIX-SHOOTER KILLER' – AMBER CITY POLICE ABOVE THE LAW?

No one else was ever tried in the murder of Maria Tarelli. The DA was replaced the following election year anyway, and the case remains unsolved to this day. But I know what happened. I was cracking down hard on the Blue Wreath at the time. I was putting their operatives behind bars left and right. I gained a reputation. Became a target. So they struck back. Sent a message.

Why couldn't they have just killed me? Why'd it have to be her?

I know the answer, of course. . . . Because why kill a man when you can destroy him?

Since the charges against me had been dropped, I still technically had a job with the Amber PD if I wanted it. I didn't. I retired. I sold our house, got a little place out in Savage Knoll, and tried to lay low for a while. Kept to myself. Did a lot of thinking and a lot more drinking until the money ran out, then started taking private work.

For years after Maria died, I couldn't read a single news article without drawing a hundred and one connections to her murder. Even after I moved back to Amber City, I couldn't take homicide cases. I kept seeing ghosts. Every killer was the Six-Shooter Killer, and I'd jump right back to trying to solve Maria's murder. Hell, I still am. I could have gone anywhere in the star system—why else would I return to Amber City?

Because this is where I have to be to catch the bastard. . . . If he's still out there somewhere.

Th factory on 105th is locked down tight, now, but it's nothing the correct tools can't overcome. Letting the locks and chains fall beside the door with my bolt cutters, I step in, turn on my flashlight, and shut the door behind me.

All I can see is what falls within the cone of my flashlight's influence. The factory looks the same as it did the last time I was here—except this time, no cops and no lights. It's black as deep space, and the darkness is made all the worse by the rainwater leaking everywhere, echoes amplified within its cavernous confines. You couldn't see somebody if he was an arm's length away, and you wouldn't hear his approach, either.

Picking my way back to the rear of the factory, following the trail from memory, I find it.

Retractable, folding fencing has been erected in a pentagon around the scene of the crime. The crisscrossing sections of the fence cast shadows of skewed longitudes and latitudes on the far walls, shifting with every movement of my flashlight. I stop for a moment and scan my surroundings to be sure I'm alone.

No monsters in here but me.

I turn my attention to the giant, rusty pallets behind the crime scene, stacked up by the killer, apparently, to hide Nathan Harland's body and moved aside by the police. These things are huge, industrial-grade pallets designed for transporting and storing starship components. Each is ten feet long by ten feet wide, made of a synthetic superalloy, and each probably weighs well over 600 pounds. They're stacked one on top of another, creating six-foot-high walls and a sort of alleyway between them. I raise my flashlight and venture between the stacks, feeling like a rat in a maze.

I pause partway down the alley. I swear I heard something other than rainwater just now—straight ahead of me, at the back of the pallets.

I transfer the flashlight to my off-hand, slipping my good hand inside my jacket to grip the butt of my .44 in its chest holster. It's already killed two men tonight. If anyone else tries coming after me, they'll get the same.

Creeping forward, I emerge from the back of the pallet stacks and find a second set of retractable fencing. For a moment, I think there must have been some additional feature to this crime scene that Albright withheld from me. Instead, I realize the fencing surrounds a piece of equipment: a shiny industrial gravjack with the Amber PD coat of arms emblazoned on the front.

I turn around, shining my light in every direction, but all I see are pallets and more falling water. No other equipment. . . . So, how'd the killer move the pallets to cover the body—?

A dull thud from the corner. The same noise I heard before, I'm sure of it.

I draw my .44. I move forward with both my arms raised in front of me, my flashlight in one hand and my weapon in the other. Ahead, I see the metal rungs of a ladder, extending upward, toward a small, boxcar-like room mounted high above the factory floor. That'll be the foreman's roost, used for supervising everything on the factory work below.

For a couple seconds, I just stand there, frozen in place, trying to hear the noise again. Strange sound. Sudden and loud. Loud enough to be heard over the water. Something falling from the ceiling?

Or something tossed this way to distract my attention?

I wheel around behind me, light and pistol held parallel, but there's nothing.

Water drips down on my head as I turn back and sneak toward the corner of the factory. I hold the pistol stiff-armed and straight ahead, already bracing for the recoil—

The thudding noise erupts beside me. I jump back, but something's right in my face, moving wildly, coming right at me, too close for a shot. I raise my gat to clock the attacker, but it just keeps going, higher and higher, thudding on the wing, sailing upward, toward a wide opening in the factory roof.

As the pigeon exits through the gap in the roof, I can still hear the thudding of its wings. I'm left watching it go, pistol aimed stupidly in the air after it.

For a little while, I stand, breathing heavily, trying to settle my rattled nerves, trying to slow my heartbeat back to resting rate. I look at the ceiling, the falling water, the gun in my hand, raised and aiming upward after the bird. . . . Upward, and at about a forty-five-degree angle. Suddenly, I'm remembering the bruises ringing Nathan Harland's neck—

A noise from the front of the factory. Not a bird. Voices.

I shut off the light and duck for cover.

"Somebody's got a light back there!"

Wilmer O'Hara.

"Police! Put your hands on your head and get down in the ground!"

Albright.

It's so black without the flashlight that all I can see now is the dull sheen of rainwater on the ladder a few yards away. The crazy thought occurs to me to climb it and hide in the foreman's roost. It's followed by an even crazier notion to comply with Albright, but I banish both from my mind. I wouldn't make it up the ladder quickly enough. And it's not that I think Jean-Luc would break up an old friendship over a little breaking and entering, but he might use this little stunt as leverage, and I don't like being on the wrong end of leverage.

I can see the cones of two flashlights bobbing my direction. I consider trying to swing wide around them and making a break for the door, but there's no way to be sure they're alone. Could be more cops outside.

Something catches my eye. A bit of streetlight peeking through a broken slat in the back wall. I jog toward it—

I can't contain a shout as my shin connects hard against a bit of debris. It falls over with a crash against the factory floor.

"Over there!" shouts Albright. "Get down, or I blow your head off!"

My shin is almost numb from the impact. Trying to ignore the pain in my knees, I double-time it toward the opening. The weathering of years, coupled with vagrant trespassing, has left an opening: a jagged, rusty corridor somebody must have wedged free a long time ago. I'm not a small man, so it takes some doing to fit through. I feel jagged metal digging into my shoulder as I squeeze through, but thankfully, the only damage is to my coat. And a little to my pride.

I stumble out, turn, and hoof it up the alleyway.

16

The driver in Taxi Cab 899 is either the same guy who gave me a lift that first night or his twin. A skinny little fellow with an Ul'ru accent, playing twangy music. Flying over the skyscrapers, I sit in the backseat, leaning back and massaging the throbbing place where I banged my shin escaping the factory. After narrowly avoiding Albright and Wilmer, I've decided enough is enough. I'm headed downtown, to the Amber City Morgue.

I need what I was promised in the beginning. A first-hand look at the body. Because things are starting to move pretty fast, and something's just not adding up. But first, I take out my datapad and prompt a number to dial. It's time to see if any of what Caesar and I discussed has sunken in yet.

Caesar answers after only two rings. "Jack. . . . How can you do such a thing?"

My brow furrows. "Come again?"

"How can you do this?"

"Caesar, I don't have the slightest—"

"You tell me to call you if I find anything," Caesar snaps. "I'll tell you what I just find. My doorman, dead! Beaten to death!"

For a moment, words elude me. Beaten to death? That guy was strong as an ox and nearly as big. If I hadn't stunned him by slamming his face off the countertop, he'd have broken me in half.

"You said you want no trouble," snarls Caesar, "but then you do this—!"

"What reason would I have to kill your doorman?" I say.

"To, to," Caesar stammers. "To send a message to tell me to spill what I know."

"Murder is not my idea of sending a message. Especially not some poor hired muscle just trying to make a living. . . ."

I trail off because my datapad's getting another call. Checking the display, I see a number I don't recognize.

"Look, Caesar," I say, "I don't know who killed your doorman, but if you value your life, close up shop and lie low. If whoever did it shows up again, I suggest you do a better job running from him than you did from me."

"Jack, what am I supposed to do with this body? I can't even move this elephant of a—!"

I hang up on Caesar and answer the incoming call.

"Who's this?" I say.

"It isn't your mother."

I don't know when or where Fox got my number, but it doesn't really surprise me. A man who makes his living in information knows how to find things.

"You caught me at a bad time, Fox," I say.

"You'll disagree when you hear what I've got to say."

"Talk fast, then."

"And the pay?"

"I'll owe you."

"I'll make a note of it. . . . Jack, Nathan Harland is alive."

I was surprised at the news of Caesar's doorman, but this one's too far-out to take seriously. "I think there's some static on your end, Fox."

"He was spotted a couple hours ago down at the waterfront. A jive club called The Holiday. Multiple witnesses."

"Who told you this?"

"A gentleman never asks, and a middleman never tells. But trust me, I don't deal in gossip. Only Grade-A stuff."

Cupping my hand over the datapad receiver, I lean forward to speak with the driver. "You familiar with a place called The Holiday? At the waterfront?"

"Yes, sir."

"Better take us that way."

There's a whir of antigravity engines and a quick, stomach-lurching change of momentum as the driver veers our cab out of the present skylane to swing around, back into the opposite lane of traffic.

"This information is clearly a work of fiction," I say to Fox over the datapad. "But I'll admit, it is perhaps interesting enough fiction to prompt my attention."

"Fiction?" says Fox.

"Nathan Harland is dead."

"Is he?"

"Yes."

"You're sure? You saw the body, did you?"

I open my mouth to tell him yes, but I have to pause here.

Because I didn't. I saw photos, sure, but photos can be doctored. Manipulated. Or fabricated entirely. I had assumed Albright ordered the body to be taken away out of professional pride. Because he didn't care for a nonprofessional like me sticking his big nose into police business. I'd have felt the same way if I were still in his position. My own personal bias and experiences filled in the gaps, perhaps incorrectly. Maybe Albright has been hiding something from me.

"Jack?"

I shake my head. "Sorry, Fox. Got to go. Call me if you hear anything else."

I cut the connection with Fox.

There's no warning. Only a ping of breaking glass, and the inside of the windshield is suddenly splattered with viscous red and gray. The driver slumps forward into the controls.

The change of gravity is immediate. The cab plummets.

The force of free fall smashes me into my seat, then lifts me up until my head bumps against the ceiling. Alarms start screaming, trying to alert a dead driver to pull the cab out of its sudden nosedive. More bullets punch holes through the windows and ricochet off the vehicle's frame as I ride a roller coaster drop straight to hell.

17

My first instinct is to try to duck and cover from the gunshots, but I haven't the luxury. Fighting the forces of free fall, I undo my safety restraint and pull myself up to the front of the cab.

Windows are popping. Broken glass showers down and floats in front of me in zero gravity. Through the bloody windshield, the world slopes away at a terrifyingly unnatural angle. Only suicide jumpers have ever seen Amber City quite like this. Crisscrossing lights of congested sky traffic are everywhere—around, in front, and below. We'll collide with another vehicle long before we reach the ground. It's a miracle we haven't hit anything already, in the three or four seconds it's taken me to act.

Grabbing the driver's body, I lift him out of the seat, deposit him in the passenger's side. I take his place and grab the controls. We're approaching terminal velocity. Instrument displays are strobing red and black. The altimeter rolls like a slot machine paying out big. I ignore all of it and pull on the wheel, trying to ease it back. Too hard and something will break or the boosters will stall. Not hard enough, and—

The lights of a skylane pass by me so close its drivers could have spit on the cab's hood ornament. My jaw is clenched tight and my teeth are grinding as I pull. I can feel the car responding, tilting under my command.

Gravity is changing. The car is leveling out, but streets and buildings are racing up at me. I watch the skylight of a low building come and go. I'm banking out of the dive, but I can see pedestrians in the streets.

We're horizontal, and I'm zooming over the streets like a daredevil on a low-level flyby. The alarms stop wailing, but the instruments are still unhappy about my altitude—twenty feet off the ground.

I turn hard to avoid a building, veer another to miss a commuter airbus. I don't have the space down here to slow this thing enough for a landing. There's only one place to go: back up.

I haul back on the wheel, harder than ever, and punch the throttle, sending the cab upward. Beside me, the driver's body moves, giving me hope, until I realize it's only his weight responding to the movement of the vehicle.

I bank hard left and thread the needle through two parallel lanes of traffic, causing vehicles to scatter in retreat as I head back into the sky. I've just started to level out when a blast of gunfire spatters the rear of the vehicle. I growl a curse that would make a space trucker blush, then kick it into full throttle. Whoever these guys are, they don't give up easily.

Glancing at the rear displays, it's not hard to spot my pursuers. Only other vehicle in the sky risking incarceration by flying outside a skylane. The headlamps hard on my tail—a big vehicle with a high hood and small, dense viewports. My cab's still holding together despite its near-death experience, but even on its best day, it couldn't outrun the rig behind me. Only a matter of time before one of their shots hits me.

I glance at the cabbie in the seat beside me. They must not have had a shot at me in the backseat, so they settled for the next best thing: killing an innocent man. Gunning down an innocent person just to get at me.

Suddenly, I'm seeing red. My blood is boiling. Bastards.

It's almost automatic. I hardly even think about what I'm doing. I draw my .44, use the pistol's nose to hammer the rest of the glass out of my window, and slam on the brakes.

Reverse thrusters roar. My cab comes to a near dead stop in mid-air, and the chase car is still coming.

I lean out the window. The wind whips furiously in my face. My entire upper body is hanging out in the open, 300 stories above the streets of Amber City. I'm an open target, but the chase car is too busy hitting his brakes to capitalize. I'm thinking of the cabbie's last words, "Yes, sir," as I draw a bead on the vehicle's driver-side viewport and empty the clip as fast as my finger can pull the trigger: one-two-three-four-five-six-seven-eight-nine.

Holes pepper the chaser's tiny viewport. Solid grouping, considering. I can't discern anything through its windshield, but the reaction is clear enough indication that at least one of my slugs hits home. The vehicle veers off course, barely avoids ramming my cab, and turns sideways into an off-kilter dive.

I pull myself back into the window, rev the boosters, and shoot skyward.

Checking my mirrors, I can see the chaser spinning in a drop, but I soon realize it's an evasion—not a death spiral. Already, the rig is starting to adjust its course for another run.

I take a sharp turn around the nearest building, then drop, laying on the cab's horn to alert traffic as I swing toward the nearest lane. To their credit, the cars around me check their brakes and swerve to make room as I shoehorn the cab in amongst them and ease the throttle down to cruising speed.

A cab behind me doesn't like my style and taps me with his bumper—probably before he notices the bullet holes dotting the whole rear of the vehicle. I slide a fresh clip into the .44.

A few seconds later, the chaser vehicle emerges from between the skyscrapers behind me like game fowl flushed from the trees. But by now I'm just another taxi in many skylanes full of many taxis. It'll be tough for him to find me unless he's close enough to see the bullet holes, and that's not going to happen because he's heading the wrong direction, following the trajectory I was taking when he last saw me.

I look at the driver lying in the seat beside me. I feel sick.

"I'm sorry," I say.

A few minutes after the headlamps of the chaser disappear, I take an exit. Toward the waterfront.

18

I leave the cab in an empty lot by the river with a nice view. I shut it off, leave the keys in the ignition, and ease the seat back so the cabbie can lie in a slightly more dignified position. His death is my fault, and leaving him like this makes me feel even worse than I already do. But I've been tangled up in too much action in the past forty-eight hours to risk being tied to this, too.

It won't take long—half an hour, maybe—for the taxi company to notice Cab 899's idleness. When they can't get through to the driver, they'll check its coordinates and send somebody to check it out. By then, I need to be gone. If I make it through the long night alive, I'll tell the authorities what happened to this man. No one should have to die in the crossfire like that, especially without his story being told.

I'm surprised to realize I'm bleeding. Several tiny cuts line my hairless head where I was nicked by flying glass. It's nothing serious but certainly not flattering, and I wish my hat hadn't been stepped on. I do my best to clean myself up. The Holiday's not far. I continue up the street on foot.

So far, six men have died in this mess. Three thugs shot dead in an alleyway, Caesar's doorman beaten to death—assuming that was related at all—the driver, and, of course, Nathan Harland. Or supposedly, anyway. Too many have died and whoever's behind it is going to have hell to pay. Or worse: me.

Partway up the street, I remember the tear in my coat where I ripped the shoulder open in my escape through the factory wall. Add to that some brownish bloodstains across the front, and this thing is probably beyond saving. Can't be seen like this. I gather the contents from the pockets and drop the coat in a nearby dumpster, thankful I've still got my blazer to conceal the akslug pistol holstered to my chest. Of course, shortly after ditching my coat, the rain starts again. I pull the lapel over and button it up to keep my tie from getting ruined. I already lost a nice one when I used it to bind the hands of that last thug in the alleyway.

I neglected to share with Albright what the lone survivor of my would-be killers said after our scuffle and before the cops showed up. He'd been a real stubborn sort of character but not very bright. It's easier to trick guys like that into talking than it is to beat it out of them. And a lot less work, even for a drunk man.

"What was that all about, gruesome?" I said as he started coming to. "You didn't like the look of me?"

"Go to hell," he said.

"No need for foul language—"

"I said go to hell. And rot there."

Then he spat on my shoes, and I was too dizzy from the drinks to avoid it. The sirens were getting pretty close by then, and I pretended to be angrier than I really was, using my opposite foot to wipe his spit from my shoe and growling, "Just what is it makes you Blue Wreath Boys such irreverent gutter trash?"

"You're a corpse, Jack the Knife!" gruesome yelled. "The old man's good as dead, ain't nothing you can do about—!"

He didn't finish his sentence because then I really did lose my cool, no pretending involved. I don't like that name. The shoe he'd just spit on came up and kicked him hard across the choppers. Before he could regain his wits, the first of the cop cars came in for a landing, and no further words could be exchanged before Jean-Luc and Wilmer arrived, turning the whole ordeal into their business. If I hadn't lost my temper, I might have gotten a little more out of him. But I still left that alley with some new information.

It was what he didn't say that spoke volumes. I had no idea if those goons were working for the mob, but gruesome wasn't a bit indignant—not even surprised—at being called a Blue Wreath Boy. He as much as accepted it as a compliment. And if my would-be killers were working for the Blue Wreath, it means Rutherford Harland's suspicions of mob involvement in the murder of his son may not have been far off.

But something else came out of it I hadn't anticipated.

The old man's good as dead, ain't nothing you can do about—!

The old man.

His meaning is clear, and it changes everything.

The usually pleasant smell of the waterfront is nowhere to be found tonight. All I can smell is the mustiness of stagnant puddles woken up by fresh rainwater, mixing to swill in the street. Alcohol-stink and cigarette smoke cling like perfume to the passersby. And up ahead, The Holiday jive club sits all by its lonesome. Little decks wrap around it and extend down the riverbanks, and under roof-cover, the party's going on. I can hear the music even from here: an up-tempo swing of quick drums, eight-to-the-bar piano, and blasting horns.

I try to focus on the music instead of the people as I push

through the crowd and approach the front door. Three large bouncers in cummerbunds and bow ties stand lazily around the door. They eye me up something fierce. Maybe it's the scratches on my head, or maybe they just don't like strangers. For a minute I think I'm about to get tossed, but I make it through the door without any trouble. Whether that's a blessing or a curse, time will tell.

The entryway has a warm, parlor sort of feel to it. It'd probably be nice, if not for the people. It's been years since I've been anywhere so crowded. Bodies are everywhere, the majority half my age or younger, drinking, dancing, and smoking. Most are sauced and still filling the tank, and it occurs to me that Fox's sources may not be as reliable as he thinks. How anybody would take notice of any one, specific face in this crowd is beyond me. But I've got to do my due diligence here. Because after my discussion with that thug in the alleyway, this has become more than just the hunt for a killer. It's a race to prevent the murder of a second target—maybe the only real target all along. The "old man." Rutherford.

I consider consulting the bartender, but one look at the queue of thirsty drinkers in the way changes my mind. I decide to case the joint instead. The music becomes even louder as I shuffle through the parlor and into a dance hall. The band must be somewhere close by, but the lighting is too dim, and I can't see much through the crowd.

A young guy spins in mid-dance and bounces off me so hard it nearly knocks him off his feet. The kid turns around, sleeves rolled up, looking sore and ready to sock whoever ruined his good time. He takes one look at me—big, scratched up, the vein in my forehead probably bulging—and he scurries off.

Deeper in the club, I find a lighted corridor and follow it to a side room where things are more my speed. There's a roulette wheel near the entrance and table games set up across the room. The guests in here are better-dressed and grimmer-looking than the dancers out there with the band. They gamble and sip drinks delivered to them on platters.

I walk in, trying to look inconspicuous. Security guards in the corners watch me. Other than that, the only eyes that seem to even notice me are soft, brown ones. Like Rutherford Harland's, yet somehow completely different. Yvonne Reed.

Mrs. Reed does nothing to give away that she knows me. After we lock eyes, she turns back to the table and pushes a pile of chips across the felt.

It's as I'm watching her that my datapad goes off. I check it, not in the mood to deal with more of Caesar's frantic rambling, but instead, the incoming number belongs to none other than Rutherford himself.

I head to the bar, take an empty stool, and answer the call.

"Yeah?" I say.

"Hello, Jack."

"Is everything all right?" I ask.

"I have some . . . news. Can you talk?"

I take a quick look around. Although the room is crowded, they're all too busy in their own affairs to pay me any mind.

"I've got a minute. Go ahead."

"Where to begin?" says Rutherford. He sounds distressed. Even more so than he was at our first meeting. "I was attempting to get Nathan's affairs in order when my bookkeepers uncovered something. Nathan was spending company money."

"Let me guess," I say. "On real estate. Under the name Royal Evening."

A pause. "You knew."

"Knowing is what you hired me for."

He makes a throaty noise. "Indeed. Does it have something to do with his death?"

"I don't know for certain yet. I should've told you about it myself, but I've gotten a little tangled up. Had a few unfortunate run-ins."

I look over my shoulder at Yvonne Reed at the card table.

Speaking of run-ins. . . .

"Mr. Harland," I say, "can I ask you something personal?"

"Proceed with caution, Mr. Tarelli."

"What's the story with your daughter?"

"Yvonne is a dear, but she's rotten. Contentious. Selfish almost beyond logic, at times. I think she has an undiagnosed personality disorder."

"Fatherly love has not blinded you."

"If only . . . It's my fault, I'm sure. I was never much of a father to her. I was already old when she was born, and before I knew it, she'd grown up and gotten married. She moved back in with me after her husband left her, and she's been here ever since, jealously possessive of my attention. Don't let her age fool you, she never really grew up. But if you're asking me if I think she's a killer, no. Imbalanced, maybe, but I don't think she's a murderer. Just a brat, not at all fit to run my companies' affairs after I'm gone. That was Nathan's destiny. But now I sit here revising my will, trying to decide whether to split up my empire, granting independence to all my subsidiaries and effectively rending a life's work . . . or leave everything to Yvonne, in the hands of a child who'd rather rip the wings off butterflies."

"Right," I say.

"I'll let you return to your work, detective," says Harland with a weary sigh. "Best of luck."

"Best to you, too."

The connection is broken, and I put the datapad away.

"I get you something, Mack?"

The well-dressed bartender is looking at me expectantly. Before I can answer, a voice from behind says, "Well, I wouldn't mind a drink."

Turning, I come face-to-face with Yvonne Reed. She's wearing a long black evening gown with a slit running from ankle to thigh. Her dark hair is done up, and her brown eyes are watching me.

"Whatever the lady's having," I say.

19

Leaning with her back against the bar, Yvonne takes a sip of her drink and studies the scratches on my head.

"My, you're a mess," she says.

"Some days more than others," I say, wondering if she heard any of my conversation with Rutherford. If she did, she's not giving it away. "How's your luck tonight?"

"Hmm?"

"The tables."

"Oh. It's been all right, but gambling bores me. Unless it's the horses."

"Come here often?"

"Are you trying to flirt with me? You must be twenty years my senior, Mr. Tarelli. Shame on you."

"Well. A beautiful woman, looking lonely—you can't blame a guy. You are alone, aren't you? Not very smart, in this part of town."

Yvonne looks around the room in an unconcerned sort of way. "You might be surprised to learn I'm not the delicate flower you think I am."

I watch her carefully as I say, "You here looking for your brother?"

It reins in her full attention, and try as she might, she can't hide that she is at once interested—yet unsurprised. I'll take that as a yes.

"You know," I say, "it took a pretty good intelligence man to lead me down here. For you to have beaten me to the punch, you must have a pretty good intelligence man yourself."

She smirks. "Who says it's a man?"

"Uh-huh," I say. "I've been enjoying your little act, by the way. My favorite part was that first night when you pretended not to know why I was meeting with your father. Anyone with half a brain could have guessed I was a detective. But you were playing dumb. You reprised the role the next day over the phone."

Yvonne downs her drink and slides the empty glass up the bar with a flick of her finger. "It's not a hard part to play. Most people assume, before I even open my mouth, that I'm a self-important, brainless twit. Growing up in my father's shadow, I learned it was easier to get ahead if I pretended to be what everybody already thought I was."

"I see," I say.

And I truly do. A smart, ambitious woman in her position might have fought to prove herself. But an uncommonly smart, deadly ambitious woman—like Yvonne—would devise a means to use her circumstances to her advantage. Play the part of the spoiled, ditzy socialite. Operate in the shadows.

"You hide the real you to get what you want," I say.

"Or need."

"So, who is the real Yvonne?"

"Getting a little personal, Jack. Only one man ever knew the answer to that question, and I guess he didn't like it much because he didn't stick around."

"Your husband clearly wasn't man enough to handle a strong woman."

"That's quite enough of that. You want to know what I'm doing down here. Well, same as you. Trying to find out if there's any stock to the rumors of my supposedly dead brother walking around alive and well."

"Have you?"

"Some waitresses say he came in wearing a large black suit and hat, acting like he was trying to hide who he was. They swear up and down it was him."

"What do you make of it?"

"You're the detective."

The bartender has returned to sit a fresh drink in front of her even though she didn't ask for one. She smiles at him, running a finger over the countertop, making little circles with her nail and looking coy.

"If Nathan somehow faked his death," I say, once the bartender's out of earshot, "then it begs the question: What reason did he have to do it? What did he have to gain from disappearing?"

"And you think I know?"

"No," I say. "But asking rhetorical questions out loud sometimes elicits useful responses."

"Well, here's one rhetorical question you haven't asked, hot shot. What if he didn't have anything to gain? What if he was in some sort of trouble and was trying to get away from it? Or what if he didn't fake his death at all, but somebody else faked it for him?"

"That's *three* questions," I say.

I'm trying to play it cool, but this woman's cunning is keeping me on my toes. It doesn't jive with Rutherford's description of her, and if even her own father doesn't know who she really is, what else might she be hiding? Is she just playing me right now? Setting my mind off after false leads?

"As for what Nathan would be doing here," says Yvonne, so low I have to lean in to hear her. "If you had done your homework, then you'd know that a few Blue Wreath agents operate out of the back room of the Holiday. And they've been staring daggers at you since you walked in."

I start to say something, but before I can get it out, she says, loud enough for anyone nearby to hear and in a much different tone of voice, "Well? Are you going to walk me out, or aren't you?"

"I thought you weren't afraid of being alone," I reply.

"Oh, I'm not. But you'll feel better knowing I get home safely."

But by now it's clear who's looking after who.

20

No one follows us out of the club, for which I am grateful.

I pay a taxi to take Yvonne home. Maybe it's a testament to her quiet intelligence that it doesn't occur to me, until she's already airborne, how perfectly ridiculous it was for *me* to pay for *her* to get a taxi.

I hail a taxi for myself and tell him to take me to 105th. Again. Maybe I'll have better luck this time. I pay special attention to the driver, and I silently pray that picking me up won't turn out to be the biggest mistake of his life. In fact, I'm paying such special attention to the sky around me—scanning for any sign of a familiar vehicle, possibly with tightly grouped bullet holes riddled across its splintered windshield—that I don't notice the trouble below.

As the cab lowers down to 105th, I realize a moment too late that there's an Amber PD squad car with its lights off sitting right in front of the factory.

I growl angrily at my own foolishness, recognizing Jean-Luc Albright leaning against the hood of the cruiser, smoking a cigarette, watching me come down. Too late to turn back now.

I pay the driver and step out into the street. As the taxi takes off, Albright makes a show of casually watching me. He's got his right hand under his coat, and he's making a show of that, too.

Little Wilmer O'Hara steps out of the other side of the cruiser. "And what do you think you're doing here?" he blurts out.

"You forgot the bolt cutters," says Albright.

"Don't own any bolt cutters," I reply. "But I could use a pair, if they're just lying around."

The looks on both their faces say they're done playing. Fortunately, I know that the best way to deal with angry dogs is to give them something to chew on.

"I don't know what the night's been like for you boys so far," I say, "but it might interest you to know that the deeper I get sucked into this thing, the more somebody seems to want me dead. In my experience, that means I'm getting warmer. It might also interest you to know there's a rumor going around that Nathan Harland is back from the dead."

Wilmer and Albright exchange a look.

"Funny you should mention that," says Albright.

"Albright, don't!" Wilmer hisses.

I watch them both carefully for a second.

"Tarelli is ex-homicide," Albright says. "I don't like breaking regulation any more than you do, Wilmer, but we could use the manpower. All three of us are working the same case, anyway. Might as well be all three of us who bring him in."

"Bring who in?" I say.

Albright gestures for his partner to answer. Wilmer sighs and says, "Nathan."

"Tell him what happened, Wilmer," says Albright.

Wilmer clears his throat. "I got a call from somebody claiming to have information relating to the Harland case. For a second, I thought it was you again. Then the guy said he *was* Nathan Harland, and he wanted to meet us at the place where he killed himself."

A crack of thunder comes echoing through the city from somewhere far away. The rain starts coming down harder. Wilmer tugs his coat tightly around his shoulders. Albright seems not to notice. He pulls out his datapad and checks the time.

"Whoever made the call," he says, "they should have been here by now. Unless it was a fake, as I suspect."

Wilmer, looking miserable with his shoulders scrunched up beneath his coat, squeaks, "Couldn't we wait inside?"

Albright sighs and starts toward the factory door, but I raise a hand to stop him.

"Your mystery caller might not like the rain, either," I say, drawing my akslug pistol.

Both men seem to agree. From a chest holster, Wilmer draws a small, boxy-looking particle pistol. Albright opens the cruiser's trunk and pulls out a double-barreled akslug shotgun, he cracks it open and slides two scattershot cartridges inside.

21

Wilmer is first through the door, eager to get out of the rain. All three of us have flashlights, and we turn them on to illuminate the immediate darkness. The factory is the same—dark, with rainwater pouring in through the ceiling and pooling all over—but somehow it feels worse in here than ever. Our triple cones of light scan the entryway like spaceport searchlights as we inch our way in.

"Think anyone's in here?" Wilmer whispers.

"One way to find out," says Albright. "Better take point, Tarelli."

"I'm flattered," I grumble.

All he wants is to keep an eye on me, of course, but I'm the odd man out, so I go ahead and step in front of Wilmer to lead the way. Albright takes position behind me, the big double-barrel cradled in his arms like a baby. Thunder—getting closer—erupts outside. I hear the rafters rattle.

Moving at a cautious speed, I pick my way toward the scene of the crime at the rear of the factory, past rusted pallets, abandoned equipment, and waterfalls of leaking rainwater. Nobody and nothing out of the ordinary to be seen, but that only goes so far in the way of comfort. Maybe it's Albright behind me, or maybe it's just nerves, but I have the profound feeling that I'm being watched.

It takes almost a full minute at our crawling speed to make it to the bloodstained floor encircled by fold-out fencing. This is where the body was found. Supposedly. I'm reminded that I never actually saw it here for myself—

"Hey! Anybody in here?" Albright's shout is so loud and sudden that it makes me jump. His voice echoes for miles, but there's no response.

"I don't know about all this," Albright growls. I'm still scanning the surroundings with my flashlight. "Beginning to feel a little stupid in here, hollering at dead people."

He's just finished the sentence, the last sentence he will ever speak, when the first shot is fired.

A bright flash of red behind me. A sound like the release of high-pressure steam.

I wheel around with my light and my gun raised. Albright's looking at me with his shoulders slumped forward like a hunchback. I can't tell if he's confused or angry or both. There are two more flashes, and two red beams of light burn out through the front of his chest and go sizzling over my head. Tiny flames jump from his jacket, trailing smoke. His body shakes. He drops his shotgun. All of this happens before I can find the form of little Wilmer O'Hara behind him, particle pistol raised, blasting his partner in the back.

Wilmer turns the gun on me. I leap sideways, hearing the hiss of a shot that barely misses. Albright, still somehow on his feet, tries to take a step at Wilmer, but it's all he's got left in him. He trips and collapses in a heap.

The flashlight has fallen from my hand. I can't see anything of Wilmer except for the beam of his own flashlight. I lunge for it, catch hold of his wrist, and twist with all my might. I feel reverberations of grinding and popping beneath the skin as Wilmer's bones break under my fingers. He screams in pain. His pistol clatters against the factory floor.

Wilmer wraps up with me, grabs my face and digs in with his fingernails, going for the eyes. My hand's still clutching his broken wrist. Discarded flashlights point aimlessly across the factory floor, but in the peripheral illumination, I can see Wilmer's face, twisted into a conglomeration of pain, rage, and desperation, as his teeth clamp down on my hand.

I throw an elbow, knocking him back a step, then swing my .44. It's too dark to see, but I can feel the impact as the butt cracks against Wilmer's temple. He makes a pitiful sound, then crumples to the ground, out cold.

I snatch up my flashlight, find Wilmer's particle pistol, and give it a swift kick, sending it spinning across the factory floor well out of reach. It's only out of habit that my body knows to do this; my mind is having a hard time keeping up. I point the light at Wilmer to confirm he's out, then turn to check his partner, but it's as I feared. Jean-Luc Albright is dead.

"Damn it all," I say.

The call was a fake, all right. That much is clear, now. Wilmer must have fabricated it and the whole story about Nathan, just to bring his partner back to the factory and eliminate him. But why—?

"Not bad."

I spin toward the voice, pointing my light and weapon toward the source of the sound, ready to shoot. Behind me, less than a dozen feet away, stands Nathan Harland.

22

"Nathan?" I say.

He's just as I remember him from the pictures: fattish, with a ruddy sort of face. Nice shoes. Black suit pants that look expensive but are badly wrinkled and nearly ruined. In his matching black jacket and tie, he looks like a corpse dressed for the casket—undead and standing right in front of me, watching me with a sort of vague disinterest. I hope he can see me all right as I slide my .44 back into its chest holster and raise both hands toward the ceiling, trying to convey a truce.

"I'm working for your father, Nathan," I say. "Are you hurt?"

Nathan watches my movements but says nothing. He almost looks disinterested, staring right through me.

"I don't know the whole story here, and I don't know what you've done, or haven't done, or why," I tell him. "But I'm no cop, so it doesn't much matter to me. Your father just wants to know what happened to you. Nobody else needs to die. Let's put an end to it."

Nathan tilts his head to look at the ground as if considering.

Whatever ulterior plans were a part of this scheme, and whether he was a willing participant or not, he surely didn't anticipate this much violence and death. Seeing what just transpired here seems to have him in a state of moderate shock. And he's not the only one. Why Wilmer would have done what he just did is beyond me. When he wakes up, I'll—

Nathan closes the gap between us so fast that I can't even finish my thought. There's no time to defend myself. In one motion, he rushes me, grabs me by my arms raised in surrender, turns, and flings me over his shoulder like a toy.

I'm airborne. Me. A six-five, 275-pound man, airborne. Picked up and tossed like a toy. How high and how far, I can't say, but I am a projectile long enough for at least one full, startling thought to cross my mind: Nathan Harland is, somehow, stronger than any man alive.

I crash-land atop the folding crime-scene fence, which buckles beneath my weight, probably saving me from a broken neck or worse. I scramble to get up, but my feet are entangled in fencing. Thunder explodes high overhead, and through holes in the factory ceiling, a flash of lightning turns the sky yellow. I can hear Nathan's approaching footsteps somewhere in the darkness.

Rolling free of the fencing, I pull a flash grenade from inside my blazer. I pop the pin. Nathan's shadow is coming straight for me. I drop the grenade and turn my head with arm raised to shield my eyes.

Even through closed eyes, I can see the flash, bright as a lightning strike, right here on the factory floor and all the more potent in this darkness. Nathan will have received the brunt of it. Even if his eyes were closed, he'd—

An explosion of sharp pain in my lower back, and I go tumbling, sliding, rolling across the factory floor. I don't know what hit me—a fist, a foot, a knee, a steel girder—but it was hard, and I know even before I've come to a stop that I'm busted up good. Something's broken in there, I'm sure of it.

When I stop rolling, I pull the .44 and draw aim into the darkness, but Nathan is nowhere to be found.

For a couple of seconds, I sit there, panting hard, grunting from the pain that each breath sets to stabbing into my back. I try to keep my arm steady as I look down the metal sights, aiming into the darkness where Nathan Harland—or whatever Nathan Harland has become—disappeared. But all I can see are shadows on shadows. A couple dozen yards away, three discarded flashlights lie uselessly on the ground, illuminating nothing but rust, the puddles on the floor, and the foot of Jean-Luc Albright's corpse.

"Damn it," I wheeze, but it's more of an automatic response than anything. I'm not even sure who I should be mad at. Maybe at Nathan for throwing me around like an irate drunk throwing his barstool. Maybe at Wilmer for showing his true colors at a moment when there was nothing I could do to save Albright. Maybe at Rutherford for sending me to my death like this. More likely, I'm just mad because I'm such a glutton for punishment.

Still no sign of any movement in the darkness. The grinding and stabbing in my back is an awful affair as I attempt to stand. It takes several tries, but it seems I was lucky. It's more pain than damage. Whatever's broken didn't cripple me. Right now, that's all that matters.

"Nathan!" I holler.

No answer. Just thunder.

I turn to look toward the front door. How far would I make it, if I tried to run? Probably not very far. So instead, I turn and head deeper into the factory, weapon raised. The broken wall panel where I escaped before. I know it's somewhere this direction. With any luck, Nathan doesn't know about it.

"Nathan!" I call out again. "I don't know what's happened to you, but we can fix it. Things are bad. People are dead. But we can still fix it. . . ."

Sneaking down a shoulder-high row of pallet stacks,

limping against the stabbing pain in my back, I keep my gun raised, tucked nice and close against my chest for maximum mobility. With every beat, my pounding heart seems to shake me from hip to collarbone.

"You've got money," I yell. "Your father's got even more. You in some sort of trouble? Even if you have to do some time, money can buy a lot of things. It won't be so bad. You'll be out before you know it, and things can go back to the way they used to be."

A rhythmic sound is suddenly echoing through the factory that stops me in my tracks. As it grows louder and longer, I finally realize that what I'm hearing is a clucking sort of laughter.

"You can't begin to understand," a voice says.

I'm looking around frantically, but the voice seems to be coming from every direction. I can't tell whether he's in front of me, behind me, beside me. . . .

"You think I don't know how these things work?" I holler, trying to get him to speak again so I can pinpoint his location. "I used to be a cop. I can help you."

"You don't know who you're dealing with . . . Jack the Knife."

And then I realize where the voice is coming from.
Above.

23

I crane my neck, searching the ceiling, and my eyes come to rest on the boxcar-like structure hanging high overhead. The foreman's roost, where supervisors once oversaw work throughout the entirety of this factory in its heyday.

No noises. No more voices. The only sound is the shuffling of my own feet—and the little sounds in my throat I can't help from making when the pain hits too badly to stifle them.

I bend over slightly, trying to stretch out my back. It's already swelling and getting stiff, but stretching only makes things worse, so I just keep moving.

Every few steps, I look over my shoulder. I suddenly realize only two of the discarded flashlights remain. Maybe Nathan grabbed the third one. Or maybe Wilmer woke up and took it for himself. Stupid of me to have left him there. I should have used his own cuffs on him while he was knocked out, but I had more pressing concerns at the time. Maybe he escaped. Or maybe he grabbed Albright's shotgun, and he's following me right now.

I'm standing directly beneath the foreman's roost. There's a lift, but it looks like it hasn't functioned in years. The service ladder—a tower of uncaged steel rising thirty feet into the air— is my only option.

I stop, taking a moment to reconsider every crazy notion running through my head. I don't know why Nathan came at me like that. He could have killed me. Now, I'm injured and outmatched, against an opponent whose abilities far exceed my own. And he called me by name. How did he knew who I am?

The front door's too risky now, with Wilmer possibly waiting there. That means I either continue toward that broken panel in the rear of the factory, or I attempt a very high climb.

I wrap my fingers around a rung of the rusty service ladder and give an experimental shake. I look up, into the darkness. As attractive as a retreat sounds right about now, I might not get another shot at getting to the bottom of this. Negotiating with Nathan, now, is about the only chance I have of figuring out just what's going on.

I holster my .44. I grit my teeth against the impending pain, grab on, and start climbing.

I don't look down. I feel rather than see my steadily increasing altitude. With every inch gained, my back hurts all the more. When I'm almost to the top, I stop and wrap my arm around a ladder rung to draw my pistol. I lick my dry lips and try not to notice how badly my hand is shaking. With weapon at the ready, I take the last few rungs slowly, peeking my head up to spy into the opening.

Nobody's waiting for me, but it's dark, and I can't see much through the opening except a big, faded glass window that once served as the foreman's view of his factory floor far, far below.

I pull myself up and step into the room with the gun tucked close to my chest.

"So the old man wants to know what happened to his boy."

I spin and duck low, pointing my pistol into the shadows. At first, I can't see him. But then, he steps forward, and I get a good view of the outline of his body—a very normal, human body, not at all indicative of the speed and strength he displayed down on the factory floor. I've got the gun aimed at his chest. I won't be caught unaware again. I don't want to kill him, but if it comes down to it, I'll learn to live with myself.

"He was gonna leave you everything, Nathan," I say. "Why fake your own death? Why cause all of this?"

"You're in over your head, Knife," says Nathan. "You're asking all the wrong questions." He shakes his head pityingly. "No matter. In the end, you're just more flesh and blood. Just another *body*!"

On the last word, he bolts. His speed is incredible, but this time I'm ready. I let him have it. I shoot him dead-center in the chest.

He staggers, but he's still coming, so I shoot again. I shoot again, and again, pumping slug after slug into his upper body. He tries to keep moving, but with every pull of the trigger, his body convulses, driving him backward step by step. Holes open across his casket-ready jacket with every shot. Yet even after nine bullets have punched clean through his body, my gun's empty, and he still won't go down. The bullets only slowed him. Now that I'm out, he charges at me like a freight train.

With a grunt of effort, I dive, throwing the full weight of my body into his oncoming feet. The pain in my back as I hit the floor makes me audibly cry out. Nathan's coming in too fast to stop. He crashes into me, tripping over my body. I feel his fingers graze desperately against my shoulder, trying to grab hold, but he misses.

His momentum is too much. His body pitches forward. A loud crash. Shattered glass rains down. Nathan goes through the window face-first, somersaults wildly, and plummets. He never makes a sound as he falls. It's almost two full seconds later—*one-one-thousand-two-one-thousand*—before I hear the thud of his body hitting the concrete, thirty feet below.

Glass is all over me. New cuts on my head and hand. I lie there, listening, trying to hear his moans of pain down below, cries for help, dying breaths—anything. But there's nothing. Not a damn thing. All I can hear is my own labored breathing.

A whole clip. I unloaded a whole clip on him, every one a potential kill shot, and he never made a sound, barely slowed down.

Thunder crashes somewhere over the city in the distance. The rattle of the rain against the roof is lessening. The storm is passing.

I stand up to the tune of tinkling glass. I try to rub some feeling into my aching back, switch out the empty clip in my .44 for a full one, and head over toward the ladder.

As I descend, my knees are shaking, both from nerves and from physical exertion. Constantly, I scan the black void below, knowing all the time that that backstabbing little murderer, Wilmer O'Hara, is still in here somewhere. All this time, he's been in on this. Probably taking his orders from the Blue Wreath. I should have been more careful.

When I finally make it off the ladder, my arms hurt almost as bad as my back. I draw my .44 and head over, scanning the area below the foreman's roost. I feel bad for what I had to do to Nathan. It's going to kill Rutherford. I did my best to reason with him, but in the end, he gave me no choice but to. . . .

Shattered glass everywhere. No body.

My gun's at the ready as I spin in a tight circle, trying to look every direction at once. I pace around the immediate area, thinking maybe he survived the fall long enough to crawl a ways before giving up the ghost. But there's nobody to be seen. He's gone.

My pulse is racing, now. A splinter of cold, venomous panic is working its way deeper and deeper into my brain. Whatever Nathan has become, I'm lucky to have survived against him this long.

In my search for a body, I've wandered close to the two discarded flashlights and their cones of light. Wilmer's gone, as I knew he would be. I turn toward Albright's body—

And almost run into Nathan.

I'm just quick enough on the draw to fire, once, before he can grab me. My aim is perfect. The shot hits him square in the jaw, blowing a hole through his head.

It only stuns him.

He takes the gun out of my hand as if I'm giving it to him as a present. Then he grabs me by the throat and lifts me with one hand.

My feet leave the ground. I can't breathe. My windpipe is being crushed beneath Nathan Harland's superhuman grip. The muscles in my neck are strained nearly to the tearing point just from trying to support the full weight of my body, suspended in mid-air by Nathan Harland who holds me up with only one arm. His other arm is dangling strangely at his side, having almost snapped completely off in the fall. Sparking wires hang out of it.

I see a gleam of metal peeking through his lapel where my gunshots hit home. And his face, where I just shot him point-blank—his entire lower jaw has been blown free, leaving only half a mouth in fact. At his cheek, a phony layer of torn skin, bloodless, hangs like peeling wallpaper from metal cheekbones.

My lungs feel like they're shriveling inside my chest. Spots are forming at the corners of my vision, but there's still enough oxygen in my brain for several trains of thought to collide into a flaming pile-up. The pallets—too heavy for a human being to have moved without equipment. The mutilated body of Nathan Harland. The bruising on the neck. The forty-five-degree angles of the gunshot wounds. . . . This isn't Nathan Harland. Nathan Harland is dead, of course. Has been all along. Killed by this thing. His own double. A bot, like the butler Hennessy, constructed to look like him. Picked up and shot at a forty-five-degree angle, upward through each eye, and. . . .

But I can't think anymore. My brain is shutting off. I'm striking him in the forearm with my fists, I'm grabbing at his hand, trying to pry his cold, robotic fingers from my neck. It's impossible.

A final idea enters my darkening mind. I stop clawing at his hand and reach instead for his damaged arm. My hand finds wires.

I barely even notice my fingers being shocked and scorched as I grab hold of a wad of wires, rip them hard, and pull them upward, shoving them into contact with the exposed metal in the face-cavity where Bot-Nathan's jaw used to be. There's a blinding flash-*crack* of grounded, electrical energy. A wild, white arc jumps from the contact point, and sparks fly. Bot-Nathan wheels back. His hand unclenches, and I drop.

To pause to catch my breath would be unwise, so I don't. I pump my legs and leap straight into the cone of light where Albright fell. Wilmer didn't take the shotgun. I grab it. I roll over to level it at Bot-Nathan, place my finger on the trigger. He's nowhere to be seen.

The shotgun is tight in my trembling hands. I suck in desperate breaths, trying to resupply my body with oxygen through a throat that feels like it just swallowed a gallon of gasoline. But despite the air coming back into my body, my vision is only getting worse. It should be getting better. Instead, it's telescoping inward into a smaller and smaller circle of vision. Something is running down behind my ear. I raise my hand and touch it. Within the tiny gun-barrel left of my vision, I see my own hand coated in sticky, red blood. Must have hit my head when he dropped me.

A whistling in my ears. No. Sirens. Lots of them. Police cruisers coming this way. And me, lying here beside a dead cop.

Even though I can barely see anything, I try to stand up, try to will my adrenaline to fuel my body. Got to get out of here. Can't let them catch me again. Can't go through another murder trial in another courtroom. Can't—

Can't feel my legs. Can't even feel my head hitting the floor as I fall forward. The last of my waning vision finally devolves to a pinprick. Blackness. Sirens all around me.

24

We met in the spring. She wore a white dress. The Songbird Diner was busy that night. I was young and mean, fresh home from the war, but I guess she didn't hold it against me. I asked her to dance. It was the luckiest break I ever got.

Over the following weeks, my life changed almost without my noticing—the way the best kinds of change always seem to occur. Years of fighting had put ice in my veins. But each night, after drinks and dancing, we would kiss goodbye and go our separate ways, and molecule by molecule, the ice melted away.

She was younger than me, but the age difference never seemed to bother her. She'd been orphaned as a child, raised by her grandmother until she was old enough to go off and study art at the university. She loved music and she loved dancing. But most of all, she loved people. Meeting them, talking to them, hearing their stories, learning every little thing about them. She was such a free spirit. Beautiful. Pure. Good. That first night, it took me all of ten minutes to fall in love with her, and every minute after that, I loved her all the more.

It all came very naturally, the changes in my life, nothing conscious or premeditated about them. I smoked, but it made her cough sometimes, so I quit. I had a bad attitude when I hung around my old buddies, and I started to drift away from them and found I didn't miss them. The hotel room I lived out of was a rat's nest, but I tried to keep it clean on the off chance she might someday see it. I lived for drinks and dancing at the Songbird. It was all that existed or needed to. On the first day of summer, I asked Maria to marry me.

"Well, of course," she said, without batting an eye.

"I promise I'll take care of you," I told her.

"I know you will, Jack," she said.

We eloped and spent three months together on the coast. Magical times. Our lives were our own. We belonged to each other and no one else.

We bought a place on the outskirts of Amber City, and I took that job with the Police Department. In the years to come, I saw some bad things, but everything was all right because I knew what I was coming home to. No matter what the scum of this city did to one another, no matter what kind of garbage I had to wade through during the day, I could still come home to her, and that made life a wonderful thing.

She loved children but for some reason never seemed interested in having any of her own. I always suspected it was the untimely deaths of her parents that had done it, drawing some subconscious association between motherhood and tragedy. But it was something else, too.

"I just can't see myself as a mother," she once said. "Can you imagine, *me*, some old woman someday, with grown-up children?"

And there it was. She wanted to stay young forever.

In a way, she did.

I just wish I had, too.

25

"Maria. . . ."

My own voice wakes me from a very bad night's sleep. Specters of forgotten nightmares tug on my consciousness. I hurt all over.

I blink hard against a stabbing pain in my head. My eyes adjust, and I'm looking at the ceiling of a dark room. It feels like a long time has passed, for some reason, but I can't remember where I am or how I got here. All I can remember is the sound of sirens.

A jail cell. How could I have let it happen? How could I have let them get me? But no, it couldn't be. It's too dark in here. They keep the cells bright—so bright that the nauseatingly sterile whiteness of the walls practically blinds you. This place. . . .

I try looking around, but moving sends a sharp pain through my back, and I grit my teeth and try not to cry out. I'm lying on the floor, shirtless, with bandages around my midsection and one big, adhesive compress stuck to the back of my head. Vaguely, an image comes to mind of sticky blood on my hand—

A noise from outside.

My eyes find a single, wooden door across the room, closed. Beyond comes the sound of approaching footsteps. Ignoring the pain in my head and back, I crawl to the door, pull myself up to a crouch, and position myself behind the hinges.

The knob turns. The door inches open. Light spills in, illuminating the empty floor. I close my hand into a fist and raise it to strike.

The door stands open, but nobody comes in.

"Do you remember what you told me about knives?"

It's a woman's voice. She's in the doorway, but she hasn't stepped in. She knows I'm standing here. In fact, it sounds like she's speaking directly to the door.

"You said that a knife is loyal," she continues, "but that never stopped anyone from cutting herself with one. I hope I haven't made that mistake tonight."

"Mrs. Reed," I say.

"I think we're past formalities now, Jack. Yvonne will do. May I come in?"

I step out from behind the door, into the light. With the adrenaline of the moment gone, this simple act pains me so much that I drop to the floor. I plop down on my oversized bottom and just sit there.

Yvonne enters the room. Her hair is tied back, and she's wearing a hardshell-plated, synthetic protective suit—the kind people wear for riding skybikes. She reaches for the light switch.

"Don't," I say. "Please. Leave it off. My head."

I can barely even look at the light of the doorway. It feels like a pressure washer is stripping paint off the inside of my skull. Mercifully, Yvonne leaves the light off and shuts the door behind her. In the half-glow of electronic displays throughout the room—didn't notice those until now—I can see the silhouette of her body as she approaches. She kneels down but keeps her distance.

"Guess I'm not in jail," I say.

"Nah," she says. "Not this time. Do you remember anything?"

"Plenty," I say.

"You've been out for a long time. Almost twelve hours."

"How am I not dead?"

"Wasn't sure if you were going to make it, so I kept you sedated until I got the internal bleeding to stop. What's the last thing you remember?"

I'm too confused to ask her to elaborate, so I answer, "Fighting a monster. Losing. Sirens. Blood. Albright's shotgun. . . . Passing out."

"I brought the shotgun with me." She gestures to the corner of the room, and sure enough, Albright's double-barrel shotgun is leaning against the wall.

"You had such a death grip on that thing, I thought I'd better bring it along."

"Why did you. . . ?" I hesitate. "How?"

"You're right, that's a much better question." She stands up, and with a sure-footed stride completely different than the

phony, gliding strut she normally uses, she crosses the room and
checks a set of monitors on the wall.

"I was listening in on police communications when
Detective O'Hara called in the murder of his partner Detective
Albright." She types something in at the monitors, steps back
when she's satisfied, and returns to stand beside me. "He said
the killer, a private investigator named Jack Tarelli, was armed
and dangerous. Then he requested backup, gave the address,
and recommended that you be gunned down on sight. You
probably would have been, too. Cop-killers don't last long,
even unconscious ones. Luckily for you, I got there first.
Brought you back here to my place."

I turn and scan the room. Workstations, monitors, and
instruments line the walls. There's only one window, and even
from the floor I can see an impressive view of the skyline of
Amber City. . . .

"We're in Rutherford's tower."

Yvonne smirks. "Let's keep that our little secret, all right?
This is where I keep an eye on things and do work that needs to
be done—the kind not everybody needs to know about. My
father pays little enough attention to me, so my secret life easily
goes unnoticed. He has no idea this place exists."

I can only shake my head. There are a hundred more
questions that need asking, but I can't decide which one should
come next.

"You know what the toughest part of everything was?" she
says. "Just getting you off the ground and onto my damn bike.
A diet would do you some good, Tarelli."

I place a hand over my bare belly, feigning indignation.
Finally, words reach my mouth. "You, uh, didn't find Nathan
tonight, did you?"

"No. . . ." Her brows furrow. "Did you?"

I ignore the question. "You told me you put on an act," I
say, my eyes scanning the equipment in the room, "but I had
no idea. A secret base of operations, hacking secure police

channels. . . . Who are you, really?"

She looks down at me. "For a start, I'm Royal Evening."

26

"Well, aren't you something," I say. "Royal Evening. It was you who made that mystery real estate purchase. With company money. And behind your father's back."

Yvonne sighs. "I wish it were as simple as all that."

She crosses the room, leans against the wall, taps her fingernails against the arm of her riding suit like she's trying to figure out where to begin. I decide to help her.

"You must have had some sort of plan lined up," I say. "You saw a financial opportunity. You needed those properties to make it happen, and you needed them discretely. So you came up here to your little secret room with your high-tech gadgets, where you do things you think people don't need to know about, and you bought the properties yourself. And in case anybody followed the trail, you left a red herring: Royal Evening. The name of Nathan's old luxury spaceliner. If somebody caught wind of something foul, they'd trace it back to him instead of. . . ."

Yvonne's shaking her head. "Wrong," she says.

For some reason, I decide now's a good time to try standing. When going about it the usual way doesn't work, I prop one knee on the ground and use my hands to boost up to my feet. I've made all sorts of unflattering noises by the time I finally stand. My lower back is stiff. There's a bandage on my hand—the spot where little Wilmer bit me—and I can feel the cooling/heating effect of medical salves at work beneath the bandage on the back of my head. Out of everything, that's the part that hurts worst. That, and my neck, from being picked up and choked. I touch my neck experimentally and flinch.

"I did leave the name Royal Evening," Yvonne says. "You're right about that. But I wasn't trying to pin anything on anybody. I was trying to be found."

I'm about to tell her how little sense that makes when she opens her mouth to keep talking.

"I've had my suspicions about Nathan for a long time," she says. "I kept tabs on him, but for years I was able to fool myself into believing he would never betray our father. He'd been distant, and he'd made some questionable decisions in the past. But working with Blue Wreath was a line I thought he would never cross."

"You think Nathan was with the mob?"

She hesitates. "Before I go any further, there are two things I want to know." She looks at me, hard. Her eyes are reminiscent of the uppity brat from that first night, but everything else—her expressions, her tone of voice, her mannerisms—are completely different. This is the real Yvonne. Royal Evening. Visible to me clearly for the first time: a cool, calculating intelligence working within the very shadows of her own opulence.

"Did you kill that cop?" she asks.

"No," I say.

"What about . . . Maria?"

I shake my head.

She looks at me a moment, then says, "I believe you."

"I don't care whether you do or not," I say.

"I can see that," she says. "That's why I believe you."

"That man you overheard," I say. "Detective O'Hara. He's the one who killed Albright, his own partner. Particle pistol. Shot him in the back."

"Why?"

"If I had to guess, I'd say he's one of those crooked cops you hear so much about. Your father suspected the mob was wrapped up in this from the start. The order must've come down to Wilmer that Albright's time was up. Maybe he was getting too close to the truth. Wilmer tried to get me, too, but it didn't go down the way he planned."

Yvonne cocks an eyebrow. "Looked to me like he worked

you over pretty good."

I scratch at a couple days' worth of facial hair on my neck. "I've been doing a lot of talking. You were saying something about your brother and the mob?"

"There's not much to tell," says Yvonne. "Nathan's worked for my father's company on the Invictus moon for years, and, as I said, I've had my suspicions about what he was up to in his spare time. He was so much older than me that we were never very close, but we were still family. When I was a girl, he'd take us on holiday to the moons of Doul. Those were the only times I ever really got to know him."

"On the *Royal Evening*?" I interject.

She nods. "After he scuttled the ship and melted it down for scrap, we hardly saw each other anymore. Then, a few months ago, I intercepted a communication sent from his personal number. He was working some inside deal on Jannix. But from a financial standpoint, that didn't make any sense—at least, not for our father's business. The whole point of having off-world operations, on Invictus, is to bypass certain planetary government sanctions—tax and legal technicalities, mostly. It would have been breaking the law to use Invictus company money to buy property on Jannix. Still, I figured he knew what he was doing. I was content to leave it alone until I stumbled on a transmission between Nathan and a guy I knew was a Blue Wreath operative. When I broke the encryption, I found out Nathan was, and had been for some time, conducting business on Blue Wreath orders. Over the next few months, I monitored him. He was in deep with the mob, and they had big plans. He was already assured to receive full ownership and operation of the Harland empire after our father passed away. Once he gained control, Blue Wreath would own everything our father spent his life to build."

"And the properties in East Amber," I speak up. "You think they were part of this business?"

"Just one of many deals Nathan had going on. Nothing

particularly special about it. I decided to use those properties to send a message. Changed the name on the title transfers as a little warning. I thought if he knew somebody was on to him, maybe he'd change his tune and back off." Yvonne stops, folds her arms. "Your turn."

I grumble a little, but I do owe her a little explaining of my own. "It'd take five men the size of Wilmer O'Hara to do all this to *me*," I say, spreading my arms to present my various wounds. "Or one very well-built bot."

Yvonne's lips part slightly as she puts it all together. Ironic, in hindsight, what Rutherford told me about his offspring: his good, hardworking boy following in his footsteps, and his untrustworthy brat of a daughter. All this time, he's had it backward.

"The rumors heard were true," I say. "Well, *I* heard it as a rumor, anyway. From my intel guy. I see now that with all this hardware, you must be your own intel guy. Nathan really was seen walking around, but not in the way either of us suspected. It was a double. A doppelganger bot made to look, speak, and behave exactly like Nathan Harland."

She looks at the floor. "So, does that mean Nathan really is. . . ?"

"I think so, yeah. I'm sorry."

"But why?"

"I suspect it was meant to effectively take his place," I say. "After you and I spoke at The Holiday, I went back to the scene of the crime to check things out. Just so happened that I got there just when Wilmer planned on offing Albright. Maybe Albright was getting wise. In any case, Wilmer pretended to have gotten a tip that Nathan was still alive and wanted to meet them in the factory. Just a ruse to lure Albright into the dark, where the real killer—the bot of Nathan Harland—could kill him, too."

"So you think the bot—the fake Nathan killed the real Nathan?"

I nod. Yvonne runs her hands over her arms, fighting a sudden chill.

"There was a lot about that crime scene that didn't make sense," I continue. "At least, not when you're assuming the killer is human. When you realize the murderer was a bot—a machine with super-strength capable of picking a man up with one hand and stacking up 600-pound pallets without the aid of any machinery to hide the body—that changes everything. I think Wilmer was going to let the bot kill Albright. But when I showed up, it threw a wrench into his plan. Albright had a nice, big shotgun that, with a well-placed shot, might have been able to take down even a bot. And he now had me—ex-cop and ex-military—there to back him up. Wilmer got nervous we might be able to take the bot down. He panicked. He shot Albright in the back. I knocked him out. Then Bot-Nathan came after me—"

There's a noise from one of the monitors on the wall. Yvonne walks over to it and checks something.

"My father," she says. "Calling for me."

"It's probably better if he doesn't know I'm here, for the moment," I say. "Until we've gotten this all straightened out, at least."

"Right," she says. She crosses the room to the door, then stops and points to a set of cabinets in the wall. "If you're hungry, help yourself to anything you can find in there. I'll try not to be too long. . . . Look at me. Hiding men in my room from my father. Someday, I ought to grow up."

She leaves me there in the dark, and for a while, I am content to just sit, enjoying the silence and rubbing my pounding head. But I'm thirsty, so I limp to the cabinet. It's full of things like food, water, medicine, and first aid supplies. But I've only got eyes for the two bottles of brandy on the top shelf.

I start to reach for the first one, but I pull my hand back. No. There's no reason for it. I don't need that stuff. Never have.

I grab one of the plastic bottles from the first aid supplies and swallow a few painkillers dry. I close my eyes. All I can see is Maria's white dress on the day we met.

"I promise I'll take care of you."

"I know you will, Jack."

I grab one of the bottles of brandy, pull open the top, and hate myself maybe more than I ever have before as I tilt it back and pour it down my throat.

27

The first time I wake up, it's to Yvonne slapping me in the face. I'm sitting on the ground, leaning heavily against the corner. She's saying something, but I can't quite make it out. She's trying to pull something away from my grasp. I assume it's an empty bottle. Then I realize, as she rips it from my hands, that it is Albright's shotgun.

I try to stand, try to say something. But all I manage to do is lurch forward. I don't have the presence of mind to catch myself, so my face shares an intimate moment with the floor, bringing into view not one empty bottle, but two.

Why now? I can't help but wonder. Why, after managing to hold on for all these years despite all the pain, have I chosen *now* to fall to so low? There were some low lows before, sure, but nothing has felt quite like this. Never have I wanted to give up so badly. Never has it . . . has everything . . . hurt so badly. Never have I wanted so badly for it all to just end.

Why now?

The next time I wake up, Yvonne is forcing my head to the side so she can clean vomit off the floor. Sweet girl. She shouldn't have to deal with this. I try to move again and realize my hands are cuffed behind my back. Smart girl, too. Saving me from myself. I wish she wouldn't bother.

28

Consciousness fades back in as I'm in mid-sip of a drink of

water. I'm sitting up against the wall, my hands still cuffed behind my back, and Yvonne is helping me drink.

"Sorry," I say.

"It's all right," she lies. "Maybe I shouldn't have left you alone like that."

"You had no reason to think I'd. . . ."

I take a great gulp of the water. My head is pounding, and my throat is very dry.

"I'm not really sure what came over me," I say. "I've had some bad nights, some close calls, especially right after I lost Maria. But I've never. . . . I've never let it get that bad before. I thought I was tougher than that."

"It has nothing to do with tough," she says. "It has to do with triggers."

"I was accused of murdering my own wife. I sat through days of a trial where my good name, the only thing I had left, was dragged through the mud. Watched as Jack Tarelli, third generation Amber PD detective, decorated war hero of Antioch, Second Lieutenant, became Jack the Knife. If that didn't *trigger* something, why this?"

"Were you there when your wife died?" she asks.

"No," I snap. "If I had been, I'd have stopped it. Or I would have destroyed whoever did that to her."

"That's what I thought," says Yvonne. "It sounds to me like you want revenge not for what happened, but because you never got a chance at a fight. You believe if you'd been there, it wouldn't have happened, right? Because you rarely lose a fight. Except for the bot tonight."

I sneer a bit. "Analyzing me, huh?"

"Maybe not," she says. "Maybe I'm just talking. Maybe I know something about it myself—don't forget that you're speaking to a woman who's spent her whole life hiding her true identity. And the only man who ever really knew me, left."

Silence for a few moments. She's now dressed in semi-formal clothing instead of the riding suit, and she takes a key from her pocket. She reaches behind me and unlocks the cuffs.

I stretch out my aching shoulders and rub my wrists. "Think I can be trusted now?"

"Do you?" she asks.

I don't answer.

"Can I ask you a question?" I say.

"You can try," she says.

"Any specific reason you chose the name Royal Evening for those title transfers? What was it, a little inside joke?"

"Maybe," she says. "I don't know if Nathan ever knew it was me or not. But I wanted him to know *someone* was watching as he betrayed his father and disgraced his name. Shortly after that, he moved home to live with us. He and I barely spoke a word to each other in that time. I never let on that I knew, though I did plan to, eventually. And if he suspected anything of me, he never gave any indication. Maybe everything that happened as a result is my fault."

I look at her. Her voice sounds sad, but her gaze remains steady and even—not a hint of breaking.

"If it's like you say," she says, "and Blue Wreath really did kill Nathan with a bot, then it probably wasn't a coincidence that they did it in that factory. Maybe the Royal Evening incident really did make him think twice about everything. Maybe Blue Wreath noticed his hesitance or saw nervousness or vulnerability in him. So they decided to . . . *replace* him. If only I'd kept my nose out of it."

It hurts my back to move, but I ignore it as I lean forward and close my arms around her. At first, she tenses up. But then there's a nearly imperceptible tilt of her head as she leans in, resting on me.

"Leave the if-onlys alone," I whisper. "They'll drive you crazy if you let them. Trust me."

I feel a movement against my chest. It's her throat clenching. Is she crying? I can't tell. Her head shifts, and she's looking up at me, and the tips of our noses are almost touching.

A crazy idea passes through my head, but I turn away from her instead of acting on it. I'm much too old for her, for a start. And besides that, Maria is the only woman there will ever be. Our life together had barely even begun when she was stolen from me. By now, she's been gone longer than I knew her. But I promised her my life, and I plan to give it to her. All of it. Maybe that seems stupid, but for some reason, it's important to me. And the most important things are always the ones that no one else seems to understand.

I study the floor for a while, feeling Yvonne watching me. Before she can say anything, I speak up.

"I guess I better tell you what I know," I say, "because if anything happens to me, you'll have to be the one to uncover the truth about this business with your brother and Blue Wreath. First thing you need to know is that this whole chain of events revolves around one very important person who remains a mystery, and I still don't have any leads."

"Who?" she asks.

"The anonymous caller. The guy who gave the cops the location of Nathan's body."

It's a struggle, but I force myself to stand. I'll have to do it sometime. Might as well be now.

"Nathan may *never* have been found if not for that caller," I say. "The body had been entombed under industrial-grade pallets to hide it. That whole district is a ghost town, and with Blue Wreath in control of Nathan's affairs, those factories would have belonged to them. If his death had gone unreported, the bot would have taken his place. That thing would have come back here. It could have been living with you, under the same roof, and nobody'd have been the wiser.

"Which brings me to my second point. . . . If control of the properties was the only motive, they could have gone about it more easily than this. No, there's a reason they needed to replace Nathan. See, a Blue Wreath boy I had a run-in with a couple nights ago told me something interesting. He said there was nothing I could do. That the old man was as good as dead."

Yvonne's eyes go wide.

I nod. "Your father. He is their target. Probably the real target all along. You said it yourself, he's stood up to the mob his whole life. Never caved, unlike most of the businessmen in this town. They have every reason to want him gone. But he's grown paranoid in his old age. Like you said that first night I was here, he's beefed up security, never takes visitors, uses a bot because he doesn't trust hired help, and hardly ever leaves the safety of his tower. But if a doppelganger bot in the shape of his own flesh and blood came waltzing in, nobody would know there was trouble until it was too late."

"There are security systems," Yvonne protests. "A bot would never get past—"

"Please. They wouldn't have gone through all this trouble if they didn't have some way around that. But it's not going to happen. Not anymore. The anonymous caller saw to that. Whoever tipped off the cops foiled Blue Wreath's plan. The body was never supposed to be found. But it was. And when that happened, their replica was good for nothing but drawing the attention of some confused waitresses down at the local club—that, and offing nosey cops, I guess."

I sigh, wishing I could have figured this all out before Albright was killed.

"So that *thing* is still out there," says Yvonne. "They could still use it somehow to trick my father."

"Probably not," I say. "Bot-Nathan almost killed me, but I messed him up pretty good, too. I imagine it'd take a while to fix the damage and get him looking convincingly human again. But that won't stop the mob. They'll still take what they want. They'll still try to get at Rutherford any way they. . . ."

NATHAN HARLAND MEMORIAL SERVICES
ANNOUNCED
Deceased's father, billionaire Rutherford

Harland, to receive guests in Amber City's
Botanical Gardens, in his first public
appearance in almost twenty years. . . .

I smile at Yvonne. "Do you think you could find it in your
heart to overlook my behavior tonight?"

She cocks an eyebrow. "In time."

"Good. Then I need your help."

29

Dawn.

It's been almost a full twenty-four hours since I woke up in
the secret lair of Mrs. Yvonne Reed. And now, after a little
healing, a little resting, and a lot of planning, I lie on an
abandoned rooftop with binoculars raised, watching the
activity in the Amber City Botanical Gardens below. I'm
wearing fresh clothes: a navy blue suit and coat with matching
hat and tie. I have a nice supply of new equipment, too, thanks
to Yvonne's resources. But out of everything, it's the hat for
which I'm most grateful. It's raining, of course, though not
bad, and it feels good to have my bald head covered again.

I scan the scene with my binoculars. The Botanical Gardens
are a staple of high society on Jannix, often used for charity
benefits and swanky parties. A thousand species of plant life
from across the star system flourish throughout the courtyard.
Statues and fountains sit tucked between tropical plants like the
ruins of some lost, jungle civilization. Beneath solar lamps,
flowers of every color and intermediate pigment bloom large
and small.

Most of the Gardens are under cover of transparent domes,
but there is an open-air section. That's where the guests and
attendants currently are. And the casket.

Black-clad funeral directors escort ladies and gentlemen of
importance—family, friends, and the Amber City elite—to
tables and seats amid flowers and ferns. They wear coats and

hats against the rain. At center stage, upon a raised dais, sits Nathan Harland's gold-plated casket. Above it is an overhanging pulpit shrouded by a silk curtain, normally used as a booth for the master of ceremonies. Today, it will be Rutherford Harland's private box.

A sliver of light is cresting the horizon through a break in the rainclouds, turning the sky blue. It's been six days since Rutherford Harland hired me to hunt down his son's murderer, and with the rise of this sun, I plan to deliver.

"You think they'll really risk it, out in the open like this?" Yvonne says.

I lower the binoculars to look at her. She's ducked beside me, watching through her own binoculars and wearing that hardshell riding suit.

"Subtlety has never been the Blue Wreath's strong suit," I answer. "They are not easily deterred. . . . Nice thing about that, though, is that it also makes them predictable."

"In front of all these people," Yvonne mumbles. "They're certainly daring."

"Far from it," I say. "They've got everything to gain and nothing to lose. But they're not counting on us."

"You've got guts, Jack."

"Don't let it fool you. *I* don't have much to lose either." I raise the binoculars back up to scan the courtyard. Two cops in dress blues and caps flank the casket. They are the only noticeable security, but several members of Harland's personal security force have taken strategic positions throughout the courtyard disguised as guests. It's an admirable effort, but against the mob, it won't be enough. "Think anyone's noticed yet that you aren't there?"

"Noticed, sure," says Yvonne. "Care? I doubt it. I'm the overlooked child remember?"

I start to say something, but then I spot shadows moving behind the pulpit curtain. "Here he comes," I say. "Get ready."

A silhouette appears behind the curtain: the old man in the

wheelchair, rolling up to take his place overseeing the ceremonies. I zoom out, trying to get a view of the entirety of the courtyard. Everyone in attendance stands out of respect for Rutherford Harland.

"You watch the box," I say. "I'll watch the crowd. Here comes the director."

Striding to the front of the dais is a man in a black suit. He raises his hands, encouraging the crowd to sit back down so the ceremony may commence.

As the guests settle into their seats, the director starts speaking. From this distance, it's impossible to know what he's saying, but it doesn't matter. I'm too busy scanning the crowd. I spot a few familiar faces—city delegates and local public figures of some importance, security in suits, trying to look casual—but still no sign of Wilmer O'Hara or his cohort, Bot-Nathan.

The funeral director steps back, then pauses strangely, looking over his shoulder.

"Jack!" cries Yvonne.

People start throwing themselves to the ground in terror as I swing my binoculars away for a view of the pulpit. The shadowed figure is swaying crazily in his chair. Bullets are ripping holes through the silk shroud. The shadow within jerks some more and falls backward out of its chair. I zoom out, trying to see everything at once. In the half-light of dawn, I see guests scattering, mouths agape with inaudible screams. The terrified funeral director is on the ground with hands over his head. Cops and private security race toward the pulpit with sidearms drawn.

"Where the hell did it come from?"

"I'm getting a call from Hennessy!" Yvonne says. I turn to look at her. She's got her finger pressed to her ear, listening to a comm feed through an earpiece. "Downward trajectory. Came from the southwest."

As I thought. They fired down, into the open-air portion of

the gardens. But I've underestimated their timing. Didn't think they'd take their shot so quickly. I point the binoculars to the southwest. Depending on the model of weapon used and the shooter's skill, it could have been a real long shot.

There are too many buildings to check them all, but in this congested part of town, there are only so many places with a clear shot. And for it to have come from the southwest, he'd have to be pretty high up.

I zoom in on a building—a tall, narrow skyscraper southwest of the gardens with a dozen old satellite bowls on top of it. I've begun scanning for a sniper among the satellites when a bit of movement prompts me to redirect my focus—not on the rooftop, but on a window on one of the uppermost floors. With my binoculars zoomed in as far as they will go, I can barely hold my hands steady enough to see the window clearly. Still, I'm able to see it before it disappears: a shadowed figure, pulling a high-powered rifle off of a tripod mount and back into an open window.

"Got him!" I growl.

Yvonne's up and running before my aching body can even get to its feet. She sprints to the rear of the roof and hops into the seat of her skybike. The headlamps come on as she revs the engine.

"Hurry up, old man!" she yells.

"Smart-mouthed little. . . ." She's putting on her helmet as I climb into the rear seat. The thing's a souped-up old pre-war model that would make a collector drool. I'm hardly even settled in when she kicks the antigrav boosters and we rocket off the roof into the sky.

I cling for dear life to the handholds as the wind whips by. The tails of my new coat billow over the back of the bike. It's all I can do not to look down.

"Came from one of the top windows, in that building with the old satellite station!" I shout at Yvonne over the roar of the wind. "We can find a way in from the roof."

She nods an affirmative and jams the accelerator, and though it seems impossible, our velocity increases. The rain smacks my face like needles, and the force of several gravities coming at me from different directions threatens to pull me clean out of my seat.

As we approach the building, I keep a sharp eye on the window. I make a mental note of the location, three stories down and five from the northeast corner.

Yvonne reduces the throttle to an idle and lets the bike drift in to hover behind one of the larger satellite bowls. Below and behind us, I can hear the sirens of police cruisers zooming into the gardens.

"This is where we part ways," I say.

Yvonne shakes her head. "You've hardly recovered from last time. You can't go in by yourself—"

"I need you to head below," I say. "To ground level. If I spook him toward you, or if he's already fast on his way down, our only chance is for you to head him off."

I detach Albright's shotgun from its cargo mount behind me, and I swing my leg over, getting ready to hop down to the rooftop. "If I need any backup, I'll call," I tell her. "If you don't hear from me one way or the other in twenty minutes . . . get out of here."

Without waiting for a response, I slide from the seat and drop to the rooftop.

I land in a crouch with Albright's shotgun tight in my hands. I look up at Yvonne on her bike. I can't see her face behind the helmet's tinted visor, but it's not hard to discern from her body language her hesitance and concern. In the end, she raises a hand in salute, slides the bike into neutral, directs it over the edge of the building, and disappears in a silent dive that makes my stomach large just to watch it.

I sigh, thankful that she agreed to leave. I've dragged her further into this thing than I should have, and I won't do it anymore. Rutherford's already lost a son. He doesn't need to lose a daughter.

I crack open Albright's shotgun and check the barrels. The rain is letting up, and I can feel the almost forgotten sensation of sunlight on my neck. I prop the butt of the shotgun against my hip and keep my finger on the trigger as I look for a door down into the building.

The satellites look rusty and unattended. Probably a decommissioned uplink station used for extra-planetary data transfers before the FTL net. I peek down a row of them as I move toward the center of the building, keeping a watchful eye on my surroundings. There, I find what I'm looking for: a doorway leading down into the building. It will be locked, but that's nothing a little elbow grease can't fix. I take a quick look over my shoulder—

The simple act of checking my six saves my life. The portly body of Bot-Nathan is lunging at me from behind.

I see his arm coming just in time to avoid it. He swings at me in a downward, lumberjack chop, the gleaming blade of a large knife clutched in his hand.

I jump back, and his arm connects with the satellite bowl beside me, instead. The knife and his hand punch a hole through the bowl like it's made of paper. I aim the shotgun.

He's even faster than I remember. He lowers his body and charges, slamming into me. I pull the trigger, but my aim has been knocked skyward. Accelerated scatter-shot fires wildly off-target, and suddenly I'm flat on my aching back. Albright's shotgun is wrenched from my grasp and flung across the rooftop.

Pain erupts in my chest, and I bite down so hard I probably crack enamel. Bot-Nathan's foot is planted against my ribcage, pinning me to the ground. I grab at his ankle, trying to force him off of me, but it's of course impossible. He's got the strength of a machine and the weight of one, too. It's like trying to tear off a car bumper.

Looking up, I see I'm not the only one who's undergone

some half-hearted repairs since our last meeting. He still wears the same bullet-shredded, black suit, but no fool would mistake this monster for a man anymore. He's been given a new arm— one that makes no attempt to bear any biological resemblance. It's bare metal like the skeletal neck of a crane, too long for his body, and wielding a triangular, three-fingered claw on the end. As for his face, the repairs were minimal. The damaged areas have been patched, he's still missing his whole lower jaw. I can see scorch marks from where I pushed the live wires into him.

The morning light reflects sharply off the blade of the very large knife in his human-looking hand. The top and only half of his mouth lifts up strangely, in the emulation of a smile. From the half-mutilated vocal box somewhere in his mechanical neck, a robotic voice growls, "JACK—THE... KNIIIIIIFE!"

He could have just shot me. Or crushed me like a bug. Or flung me off the roof. Or picked me up with one hand and blasted me at close range half a dozen times, like he did to Nathan Harland. But it seems that even bots carry some notion of irony. Bot-Nathan raises the knife.

30

My ribs feel like they're about to pop beneath the machine-man's weight, but my hands are free at my sides. As Bot-Nathan winds up for the death strike, I draw the particle pistol strapped to my calf.

I fire twice before he can react. Two red-hot blasts of concentrated radiation streak into him. The first hits his wrist and burns straight through it. I see the glint of the knife pinwheeling through the air, leaving him brandishing nothing but a handless forearm. The second blast burns a hole through his neck.

He kicks my weapon-hand before I can fire a third shot, and it's like getting hit with a sledgehammer. As the pistol flies from my grasp, I'm shouting in agony. He's just broken the fingers of my good hand. All of them. At once.

He bends down to grab me, but his head flops unnaturally to the side. The damaged half of his neck is a crater of glowing, superheated metal. He takes an awkward step, like a man fighting dizziness, and his head hangs like a flower on a broken stalk.

His sideways step frees me from his weight. I scramble to get to my feet, trying to remember where the shotgun went, but before I can take more than a single step, the claws of his extra-long arm grab my coat, pull upward, and toss me.

It's my second experience being unwillingly airborne in a relatively short period of time. For a frightening moment, I think he may have actually tossed me all the way over the side of the building. My arms flail in a pathetic attempt to adjust my landing, but little can be done. Instead of going over the edge, I land sickeningly flat on my back, right in the center of a satellite bowl. The impact is gut-wrenching. My head strikes hard against the bowl, and stars flash across my eyes.

The wind is knocked out of me. My lungs heave and groan with the effort of drawing breath. High above, the sky is clearing—turning a brighter and brighter shade of blue with the dawn. And what do you know, it's not even raining anymore. But dark clouds are still swirling before my eyes, darkening the dawn back into dusk, eating away at my vision, swirling, suffocating all consciousness. . . .

"I promise I'll take care of you."

"I know you will, Jack."

Blinking rapidly to clear the blackness, I hear Bot-Nathan coming for me. The clanking of strangely illogical steps, like a drunk on a massive bender. Weird, animal sounds are being emitted from his robotic voice emulator. Seems he's not sure where I landed.

I move my legs, testing to see if they still function. Success. Next, I test my arms. I slide them against the bowl. My hand brushes up against something that feels like cold, human flesh.

I raise my head to look at it. It's not human flesh, but I'll admit it is a convincing copy. Bot-Nathan's dismembered hand is lying beside me in the satellite bowl, and still clutched in its dead, human-like fingers is the knife.

As quietly as I can, I pick up the dismembered hand and use my unbroken fingers to peel the robotic digits away from the knife handle.

A squealing, metallic screech. I look up and see one of the smaller satellites being pushed clean off its mounts, just a few yards from me. Getting warmer.

I freeze in place. Just over the lip of the bowl, I can see the top of a sideways-hanging, human-like head moving in this direction. He's right in front of me, though he doesn't know it yet.

I pull the knife free. I see the head turn to the side, and I take my chance.

I haul back and toss Bot-Nathan's disembodied hand in a neat arc, forward, and high above him. It lands in the pit of a satellite bowl behind him with a nice, rich *GONG*.

Bot-Nathan wheels toward the sound.

I pounce.

Until I try, I'm not even sure my body is capable of doing what I'm about to do. It's far from graceful, but I manage to jump over the side of the satellite. The bot that killed Nathan Harland is looking the wrong way at the wrong moment.

I hit him in the back and latch on with all my might. He roars with a robotic objection, flailing his arms in an attempt to throw me off. I wrap my arm around the top of his flopping head and wrench backward until his synthetic eyes are looking up at me.

"*JAAAAACK*!" he wails.

"That's right," I say. "Jack the Knife."

I plunge the blade into the remains of his robotic neck to the squeal of metal-on-metal. Sparks fly. Electricity cooks my fingers. He's still trying to grab me with his claw as I pull sideways, hard, wrenching the knife with all my might across his metal throat. The knife loosens his neck. Brute force does the rest.

Pulling his head off is like harvesting a stubborn radish. A tail of a severed, mechanical spinal cord trails out with it, spilling gears and wires of dislodged, robotic viscera. A crackle of electrical energy. Lubricant fountains from the neck. The body takes a step, then drops to its knees. I step back. There's a whirring and hissing of dying machinery, and for a moment I think the body is going to explode. Instead, it just falls forward and crashes to the ground.

31

I stand there, holding Bot-Nathan's head by a fistful of hair, feeling oddly like a child with a broken toy. I watch the body for signs of life, but it doesn't move.

For a few seconds, some handicapped processing power remains active in the head. Brown eyes—manufactured to look so much like Rutherford's and Yvonne's—glare at me. The half-mouth tries to speak to me.

I drop the head. It whines on the ground with angry, meaningless syllables. Then even this fades away. Still, only after some experimental kicks am I satisfied that Bot-Nathan is really dead for good.

The sun is well over the horizon by now, and the skies are clear and wonderful. I'm tempted to call Yvonne, to have her come and pick me up so we can high-tail it out of here and leave this whole business behind me. I got the killer, after all. Mission accomplished. My work is done. But I still need the rifle that was fired from the window. I'm currently wanted by the police for Albright's murder, and what with it being little Wilmer's word against mine, my only chance of clearing my name is being thorough. Documenting every piece of this puzzle.

I head toward the doorway—a small, shed-like structure set against the north wall of the building—swinging wide to retrace my steps in search of a weapon, either my kicked particle pistol or Albright's shotgun. I'm still carrying Bot-Nathan's knife in my uninjured hand, but I'll feel better with something a little more substantial.

I'm trying to ignore how injured I really am, but it's all I can do just to put one foot in front of the other. My back hurts. My ribs hurt. My knees hurt. The broken fingers of my good hand are swollen, crooked, painful. What I wouldn't give to be a couple years younger right about now.

I spot Albright's shotgun. I'm about to pick it up when my datapad rings. It's an effort just to pull it from my jacket pocket. I check the display, see that it's Yvonne.

ZIP.

A snap of sparks. The top half of my datapad explodes. I drop the rest in surprise.

"Hands up."

I turn toward the voice.

ZIP.

A puff of dust erupts as a hole is blown in the ground beside Albright's shotgun, dangerously close to my left foot. I still don't put my hands up. I won't give him the satisfaction.

Little Wilmer O'Hara is about ten yards away, standing on top of the shed-like structure where the building stairway meets the roof. Propped in his arms is a large, high-powered rifle. His head is cocked to the side, watching me through the scope. His trigger finger sticks out from a wad of bandages wrapping the wrist I broke in the factory.

"Good morning," I say.

Wilmer works the bolt, feeding the next slug into the chamber. "Hands up, I said."

"Nah. No point," I say. "If you were just going to shoot me, you'd have shot me in the back just now. Like you did to your partner."

"I'm not fooling around, Tarelli," he says. "Drop the knife and put your hands up."

"You *can't* shoot me, can you Wilmer? Because if my body turns up with bullets in it matching the ones used to try to kill Rutherford Harland... well, people are going to get very suspicious."

Wilmer tilts his head out from behind the scope to look at me with both eyes. "What do you mean, *tried*?"

"You Blue Wreath boys are all the same," I say. "Always too eager to pull the trigger. Guess it never occurred to you that it might be a decoy behind that curtain."

Wilmer puts his eye to the scope again. Behind it, his cheeks turn red.

"Aw, what's the matter, Willie? Did I ruin your game?"

"Don't think I won't shoot you anyway," Wilmer says. "I'll figure out some way to explain it. See, the joke's on you, shamus. We'll get the old man eventually. As for you, here's the way the story's gonna go: Rutherford hired Jack the Knife, the wife-killer cop who walked, to try to catch his son's killer. But a loose cannon like the Knife—turns out, his same old history of violence tragically repeated itself. Not only did the Knife shoot Detective Albright when he got in his way, but with the cops bearing down on him, he tried to erase his connection to the case entirely. He got himself a high-powered rifle, climbed up to a sniper's roost, and tried to kill Rutherford." His lips peel back in a smile. "Then he jumped."

"A little melodramatic," I say. "Not to mention it's full of holes."

"And I'll be the first one to point that out," he replies. "May even launch a full investigation into the matter, in honor of my fallen partner. People already think you killed your wife. The public can't resist a recurring villain."

I turn slightly, taking in my surroundings. The shed-like structure Wilmer stands on is set along the edge of the roof, and I'm near the corner—only a few steps from the precipice of a 200-story drop.

"Go on, shamus," hisses Wilmer.

ZIP.

Another puff of dust, inches from my toes.

He's smiling wide as ever as he works another slug into the chamber. "Jump."

32

I look at Wilmer, look at his rifle. I'm only about ten yards away from him, and at close range, it gets tough to keep a moving target within a high-powered scope like that. But walking is difficult enough for me at the moment. No way I could move fast enough to charge him without getting a new hole to breathe from. I could try. Might get lucky. But it's too desperate. Not my style.

Mentally, I'm trying to count the minutes since I arrived on the rooftop. Some backup would be nice, but if Yvonne flies up here unaware of the danger, Wilmer's going to have a clear shot at blowing her out of the sky.

"I'm losing patience, Jack!" Wilmer shouts. "Take a walk!"

By the tone of his voice, I know he isn't bluffing. With each second, the truth is no doubt sinking in, in his brain—the reality of how bad his situation has become. He doesn't have a handle on things anymore. How's he going to get out of here today? And when he does, how's he going to explain all this to the cops? Forget the police; what's the Blue Wreath going to do to him if they decide their inside man is no longer an asset and has become a liability? It's all spiraled beyond his control, and he's getting nervous. And nervous, at the trigger of a gun, is more dangerous than mean or angry any day of the week.

I'm still holding the knife. I squeeze its handle, wishing it was something more useful. Ahead of me, I notice something on the ground. A little flake of yellow hovering over the rooftop like a fairy. It's the opposite of a shadow: a reflection of morning sunlight, caught and concentrated into a tiny square of light. The reflection of a blade.

I look up at Wilmer. In my peripheral vision, I experiment

with the refracted sunlight, tipping the knife back and forth ever so slightly. The yellow flake follows my movements around on the ground between us.

"Only one of us is leaving this rooftop alive," I say, stalling for time. "I can see that, now. But before that happens, maybe you'll answer a question for me, one homicide detective to another."

"Try your luck, if you want," says Wilmer. "But I suggest you walk while you talk. Go for that gun, and I'll blow your brains out."

I take a step backward—stepping over Albright's shotgun—to make him happy. "You said a moment ago that people *think* I killed my wife. . . . I'm assuming you would have worded that differently if *you* thought I was a wife-killer. So my question is, are you just giving me the benefit of the doubt, Wilmer? Or do you know something?"

I tip the knife upward slightly, letting the visible beam crawl up Wilmer's pant leg, toward his upper body.

Behind the scope, he shows all his teeth. "Being a 'Blue Wreath boy' does have its advantages," he says. "Sure, I know the truth. In a funny sort of way, this all fits together."

I tilt the knife even farther upward, going slowly so as not to alert him. The light is on his chest now.

"Yeah," says Wilmer. "Nash would get a real kick out of this."

My heart nearly stops.

"Nash?" I say. "Who is Nash?"

"Tacitus Nash," says Wilmer. "Why he's—"

Sirens in the distance. Getting closer. Wilmer's smile fades to a look of worry, and he fires at my feet again. ZIP.

"Now, Jack," he says.

"Who is Tacitus Nash—?" I start to say, but he works another round into the chamber and shoots again. ZIP. The ping of a ricochet.

"Jump!" he yells.

ZIP. The bullet hits the ground near my feet. The sirens are getting closer.

Reload. "Now!" he snarls through gritted teeth.

ZIP. This time, I feel the slug tear through my shoe.

Reload. He shifts the rifle up. Its barrel quivers with his nerves. It's aimed right at my face. He screams, *"Do it!"*

"Fine," I say.

I tilt the knife.

The beam of light lands squarely within the glass circle at the end of his scope. Wilmer squeals like a woman, yanking his head away from the scope involuntarily. To the naked eye, that little reflection would be an annoyance. Through super-magnification, it's got to hurt.

Wilmer fires in desperation. The bullet hits me in the shoulder, spraying blood. My body spins slightly from the punch of impact, but I manage to remain standing. Thankfully, adrenaline dulls the initial pain.

I drop the knife. It's too painful to move, so I just wedge my foot under Albright's double-barrel and kick upward. I catch the shotgun in my good hand. Wilmer is still working the bolt for another shot, blinking frantically against the blindness in his good eye, as I pull the trigger and fire from the hip.

The blast hits Wilmer with the force of a low-flying airship. He makes a strange little noise as it lifts him an inch off his feet. The rifle falls out of his hands as he goes backward, over the edge of the shed, tumbles. . . .

And keeps going, over the side of the building.

I hear him yelling long enough to know that the shotgun blast didn't kill him outright. It's a long fall to the streets below—plenty of time for him to think about the totality of his failure.

I drop the shotgun. It lands with a clatter beside the knife. Searing hot pain is pulsing in my shoulder, and my coat sleeve is soaked and dripping into a widening, shockingly large puddle on the rooftop in front of me. Sirens are wailing, close and getting closer. Carefully—oh, so carefully—I get down on my knees and do my best to put my hands behind my head, and I wait for the cops to arrive. I've lost my hat again in all the commotion. The sun is warm on my bare head.

33

The viewport from Rutherford Harland's observatory is no less impressive in full daylight. Across a blue, cloudless sky, the sun shines over the skyline. I lean on the balcony railing, my broken fingers splinted and wrapped, my arm done up in a sling. My good hand clutches a cane. I don't like having to use it. Makes me feel like an old man.

Beside me, Rutherford is quiet. I can't help but feel partially responsible, given all he's been forced to contend with over the past forty-eight hours. He'd been hesitant, at first, about my plan to stage his public appearance and use Hennessy as bait to catch the killer. I think the idea of his son's funeral—phony or not—becoming a scene of violence gave him trepidation. But, oh, how he enjoyed the idea of tricking all those high society types into thinking he was dead for a few hours.

As far as Harland knows, Yvonne had no part in any of it. She asked me not to out her as Royal Evening, and it was a request I felt obliged to honor, given that she saved my life. Twice, really.

But her other request, that I keep my mouth shut about Nathan and let the old man go on believing the best of his son. . . . That, I could not do. It was a question of professional ethics. In the end, I had to remind myself of what Rutherford hired me for in the first place: to find the truth. I can leave out certain elements of the truth that I found, but I refuse to deceive him. I had to tell him what his son had really been doing, no matter how bad it hurt.

I take a sidelong glance at Rutherford hunched over in his chair beside me. He initially seemed appreciative of my honesty, but I can tell the news isn't sitting right with him. I just hope

A KNIFE IN THE DARK

he can someday find it in his heart to forgive Nathan.

"I trust you're satisfied with your bonus?" Harland says suddenly.

"You know you didn't have to do that," I say.

"Nonsense. You deserve more, probably, but I didn't get to be where I am today by being frivolous with money. . . . Tell me. Was he very convincing? The double, I mean?"

I think I know what he's really asking: Would the plan have worked? Could Bot-Nathan have really fooled security, gotten up here, and killed him?

And could it be attempted again?

"Tricked me, at first," I answer. "But, of course, I never knew the real Nathan. I have a feeling you wouldn't have been fooled for a second."

But a second, I know, is all it would have taken.

Steady, measured footfalls echo through the observatory as a straight-backed little man enters. He walks up the balcony with a silver platter balanced on one hand. He arrives before us and bows, presenting the tray. There are two glasses on it. It's that expensive scotch from the first night. Delicious stuff, really.

Rutherford takes one of the glasses. I reach for the other. My fingers hover over the rim for a moment. Then I pull my hand back and clear my dry throat.

"None for me, thanks."

"Yes, sir," says Hennessy. He looks at me—no, through me—with those lifelike bot eyes.

"Are you recovering all right, Hennessy?" I ask.

"All systems fully functional, sir," Hennessy says. "In fact, I personally conducted all the necessary repairs."

"A DIY job, eh? Well, you made a perfect stand-in for your boss. I hope you didn't get hurt too badly."

"The placement of the would-be assassin's gunshots, while almost certainly deadly to a human, resulted in only minimal damage to my body. Any systems with temporarily impaired functionality were quickly rerouted to other processing centers, maintaining operation with nearly 100 percent effectiveness. Much harm can befall a bot before its functionality becomes jeopardized."

"You're telling me," I say.

I'm reminded just how lucky it is that I managed to take Bot-Nathan out. His remains were about the only thing that kept the police from tossing me behind bars. Hesitant as they were to believe the story about Wilmer killing Albright, it didn't take long for the pieces to start falling into place. No doubt they'll be calling to ask me some more serious questions before long, but that's all right by me. I'm just thankful to have had my name removed from the most wanted list.

"By your count, Jack," says Rutherford as Hennessy bows and excuses himself, "how many died in this chain of events?"

I exhale long and slowly, trying not to forget anybody as I rattle them off. "Well, Nathan was killed by the bot. Four Blue Wreath hitmen tried to take me out when I took an interest in the case, and only one lived to tell about it. A cab driver was killed in the crossfire during another attempt to take me out. I'm assuming it was the bot that time, having followed me after my return visit to the crime scene. But I also learned that an employee of a friend of mine was killed. A doorman, beaten to death shortly after I visited him. In hindsight, I think that was the bot, too, which means he had been following me even longer than I thought. It was either to send a message, or the bot was trying to get information about me. I've spoken to my friend since, and he's set up shop in a new part of town, trying to leave his past life behind.

"The cabbie is the one I feel most badly about, but Detective Jean-Luc Albright is a close second. He didn't like me much at first, but I wouldn't have either, in his place. He was a good man, just doing his job. When we entered that factory to search for Nathan—supposedly—Jean-Luc was shot in the back by his partner, Wilmer O'Hara, who'd been working for the mob all along. For that, I made sure to take care of Wilmer personally. He's the one who tried to take you out at your son's memorial service, and he brought Bot-Nathan along with him for protection. They found Wilmer's body on the street after a very long fall. . . . So that brings the total to eight men. I guess nine, if you count Bot-Nathan."

"I don't," Rutherford snaps.

"Well I do," I say. "He was the hardest one."

Despite everything, Rutherford's mustache twitches in amusement.

"I'm just glad you didn't end up on that list, Mr. Harland," I tell him. "Blue Wreath lost this time, but they don't give up easily. I suggest you hire some extra security around here. Lie low—even lower than before. . . . The funny thing is, you and I almost surely wouldn't be talking right now if not for a certain phone call."

"Ah, yes," says Rutherford, leaning back in his chair thoughtfully. "The anonymous tip that led the police to my boy. You mean you never found out who made the call?"

"Not yet, but when I get to the bottom of it—"

Rutherford wakes a dismissive hand. "I have other people I can ask to look into that. I'm sure it has something to do with the internal politics of this Blue Wreath syndicate. I just cannot believe they would go to such lengths. Killing my family just to get to *me*."

I swallow hard. "I know the feeling."

"Hmm, yes. . . . I have been thinking. There's something else I would like you to have."

"Mr. Harland, you've already given me a bonus—"

"Not money, man. A real, tangible token of my appreciation. Hennessy."

"Your butler bot?"

He nods.

"But you've got no other servants up here. Who's going to take care of you?"

"I've got other, less advanced machines to help me. Plus, I've got Yvonne. I know it may sound strange, but she impressed me through all this. She kept to herself, mostly, but she managed to keep an astoundingly level head. Never thought I'd be able to say as much about such an excitable, dramatic child. Perhaps, if she continues to prove herself, she could become trusted to take over after all."

At this, I can't contain my smile. "But Hennessy? Really, I don't have any use for—"

"You're taking him, Jack, and that's final," Rutherford cuts in. "Do with him what you want. Wipe his memory and flip him for a profit, for all I care. Toss him in the scrap heap. Just get him out of here."

Ah. Now I see.

"That's extremely generous of you, sir," I say.

"Well, I owe you an awful lot," he says. "If you ever need a favor. Or if you're just in the neighborhood and feel like keeping an old man company."

I extend my good hand. "I'll be in touch, sir."

He smiles and grips it gently.

34

Yvonne is in the library with an open book in her hands. The curtains are thrown wide, and light spills in, turning the dark and dreary library I remember into a spectacular altar to the sun. She wears an unassuming formal blouse and skirt, but it looks very unnatural on her, now that I've seen her in her true element.

I have to lean heavily on my cane with every step as I enter the room. Yvonne shuts the book and crosses the library to meet me, skirt flowing behind her.

"Were you surprised by your gift?" she says.

I raise an eyebrow suspiciously. "It was your idea, wasn't it?"

She stops in front of me, shrugging in a demure sort of way.

"I may have dropped the suggestion in passing. My father has soured a bit to the idea of having a *bot* around the house. Understandably. And given the constant abuse you seem to enjoy putting yourself through, you need someone looking after you. Or at least to take care of you when you have one of those . . . bad days."

"I think those sorts of bad days are behind me," I say. "Still got too much work to do, you know?"

She smiles. "Good. Still, a little extra help never hurt anyone. I can't always be there to pull your ass out of the fire."

"But if I ever need a ride?"

"You've got my number."

I smile. "You know, the real Yvonne is all right. Without her, I'd really be up the creek right now. It's—well, frankly, Mrs. Reed, it's been a long time since I had a friend."

"Me, too."

"Maybe if I wasn't so old and broken, maybe. . . . Well, a beautiful, intelligent woman like you, you can't blame a guy for wondering what could have been, if only we'd met in another lifetime."

She walks closer, stands on her tip-toes, and kisses my cheek. When her lips leave me, she tilts her head, whispering into my ear, "The if-onlys will drive you crazy if you let them."

I close my eyes. They're still closed as I listen to her footfalls drifting slowly away across the library.

"Sir?"

I open my eyes and turn. Hennessy is waiting in the doorway, my coat and hat in his hands. I take them and put them on.

Turning back toward the library, I find Yvonne watching me. I tip my hat to her. "Thank you for a lovely Evening."

She smiles.

I leave with Hennessy following me down the hallway.

"You get everything taken care of?" I ask.

"Yes, sir," Hennessy says. "The ownership of one

EnnterTech Personal Service Bot has been transferred in title from the party of Rutherford Harland to the party of Jack Tarelli. Now reporting for duty, EnnterTech Personal Service Bot, 'Housekeeper' Series, Model Number 07.11.1, Call Letters HN-SC, serial number—"

"HN-SC," I say. "Henn-ess-see. Oh, I get it."

"If you would prefer a different name—"

"Nah, I kinda like it."

As we exit through the big doors with the word *Harland* across the front, I casually slip my hand inside my coat and rest it on the new akslug .44 in my chest holster, watching Hennessy carefully. I wait until the doors have rolled shut behind us to ask him the question I've wanted to ask for days.

"It was you, wasn't it?"

"Pardon me, sir?" Hennessy says, and if he were human, I'd say he was faking innocence.

"Nathan wasn't stupid," I say. "He managed to pull the wool over Rutherford's eyes and hide all his dirty business deals. He probably had no idea what he was walking into when he went down to the factory on 105th that night, but he certainly wasn't dumb enough to go anywhere in a neighborhood like East Amber alone. Still, he couldn't risk anyone finding out about his secret dealings. He needed backup. Backup that wouldn't talk." I shrug. "If it were me, I'd bring the butler-bot."

I'm leaning on my cane with the elbow of my bad arm. It hurts, but it gives me the freedom to use my free hand, under my jacket, to slip the .44 from its holster and caress the trigger guard with my fingertip. Hennessy hasn't so much as moved a synthetic muscle since I began speaking.

"Correct me if I'm wrong," I say, "but I believe a change of ownership means you're now obligated to answer all my queries to the best of your knowledge. First question: Are you now, or have you ever been, operating under the orders of the Blue Wreath syndicate?"

"No, sir," he says immediately.

I tighten my grip on the .44. "Next question. What were you doing with Nathan Harland on the night he died, and why didn't you tell Rutherford what happened to him?"

This time, it takes a moment for Hennessy to answer.

"Had Rutherford Harland asked me directly, I would have been obligated to tell him everything I knew," says Hennessy. "However, I was also specifically commanded by Nathan Harland to tell no one where we went that night, especially his father, out of concern for his safety."

"Rutherford is your owner," I say. "Why would you take orders from Nathan?"

"My primary function under Rutherford Harland's employ was expressed as *the protection of the Harland family*. When Nathan asked me to accompany him that night based on an expressed concern for his safety, to refuse would have been against that function."

"And Rutherford wasn't suspicious that you left the tower?"

"It was early evening, and I am usually tending to cleaning duties during that time. Rutherford rarely calls on me during those hours."

"Okay, so what exactly happened?"

"Nathan Harland commanded me to accompany him to a business meeting as his personal bodyguard. I used the family vehicle to fly Nathan to the specified address, a condemned factory in East Amber. He asked me to wait in the vehicle and watch the street for anything suspicious while he stepped inside. I now suspect he was doing something he did not want me to know about. Nathan entered the factory, and I waited, as ordered. Several minutes passed. I saw no one emerge from the factory during that time. I finally decided to forgo Nathan's orders, suspecting something had gone wrong. I entered the facility.

"Inside in the factory, my bioscanners indicated that

Nathan was under a pile of large, metal objects stacked on top of one another. All his vital signs had ceased. I rang the authorities to tell them where they could find Nathan Harland's body—without giving them my name, of course— and I drove home. Nathan had told me, prior to all this, that I was, under no circumstances, to tell anyone anything about it—neither where we were going that night, nor that we had gone *anywhere* at all. As I have previously indicated, I would have been obligated to break this command, had Rutherford asked me about it directly, but, as he did not—"

"You don't think," I interrupt, "that under the circumstances, keeping all this information from Rutherford was unwise?"

Hennessy crosses his arms behind his back. He sighs— which is almost funny, given that he has no lungs. Amazing the lengths they'll go to, to make these things seem real. Someone ought to tell them to dial it back a bit.

"I am aware of a phenomenon that humans call *hindsight,*" says Hennessy. "In *hindsight,* my primary function could have been better performed had I disobeyed Nathan Harland's last orders. I certainly would have done this, had I been privy to knowledge of his illicit activity with the Blue Wreath crime syndicate, as this would have rendered 100 percent of his orders null in void. But, may I remind you, I am a machine. A machine's outputs are governed exclusively by its inputs. I was acting under the impression that I was following perfectly legal and ethical orders that were simply beyond the comprehension of one in such a lowly position as me. I see now that I made a terrible error in my reasoning, thereby endangering the Harland family and miserably failing in my primary function. It occurs to me that I should be melted down. I can recommend several top-notch deconstruction facilities, sir."

"I . . . don't think that'll be necessary," I say as I remove my hand from my jacket. "It's a bit of a runaround, but I guess I understand. You weren't the only one working with limited . . .

uh, inputs. In the end, it was your anonymous call that saved Rutherford's life, so, in a way, you did exactly what you were meant to do. You should feel good about that."

He doesn't *feel* anything, of course, but the resulting grin on his synthetic face is well emulated. "I do feel a little better, sir," he says.

Bots.

"Let me save you the trouble of any future reasoning," I say. "Your only function is making sure I know everything you know, regardless of whether you *think* I need to know it or not. So you just talk until I tell you to shut up. All right, Hennessy?"

"Understood, sir," says Hennessy. "Would you like to include your personal defense and safety as part of my primary function?"

"Are you any good at that?"

"Oh, very good, sir."

"Better do that too, then. As far as it is within your power, make sure I stay alive, okay?"

Hennessy bows a little. "I hope I will perform admirably, sir."

"You and me both, pal."

My datapad buzzes in my coat pocket. It's a smaller, slightly more powerful model than my old datapad—the one Wilmer shot in half. I've barely used it yet. I'm getting an incoming call from an unlisted number.

"Yeah?" I answer.

"My, my, Jack!" says the voice on the other end. "It sounds like you've been busy."

Fox. I thought so. "Busier than I'd like," I say. "How about you?"

"Oh, I never take a day off, but I'm extra busy today. A lot of my clients want to know the inside story about the assassination attempt on Rutherford Harland. I'd kind of like to hear the full story myself."

"That why you called? To purchase the serial rights?"

"Nah. I've actually got a piece of information I thought *you* needed to hear—you can just owe me, all right?"

"Fine."

"A few of my contacts inform me that the Blue Wreath syndicate just posted an illegal underground bounty on the head of Jack 'the Knife' Tarelli for 25,000 creds. Last known location: East Amber. Wanted dead or alive."

"Took them long enough," I say.

"Ain't exactly chump change. You might want to plan accordingly."

I chuckle a bit. "You want to hear my idea of a plan? The other day, I decapitated a bot with an assault knife and my bare hands. And if you tell your clients anything about Jack the Knife, I'll do the same to you, Fox. And that is a solemn promise."

There's a pause on the other end, followed by a throat clearing sound.

"You, uh, really are embracing that old nickname, aren't you?" says Fox.

"What can I say, it's grown on me. And one other thing, while I've got you. I need some information. . . . Everything you can find on the name Tacitus Nash."

"I'll look into it," says Fox. "Talk to you later, buddy. Keep your head down."

"Keep yours down, too. Buddy." I hang up. I turn to Hennessy and shrug. "He's a good kid. Just needs to be reminded who's boss sometimes."

"I see," says Hennessy. "And this Mr. Nash. Someone you know, sir?"

The elevator doors roll open. I hand Hennessy my cane and step out without it.

"Not yet," I say. "We'll soon change that."

Jack the Knife
Returns in:

A KNIFE IN THE DARK: ALLOYHEART

What did you think of the book? Text me at:
814-499-1311
Yes, this is a real number. No, it's not a promotional thing. I
just want to know what you think.

Books by Corey McCullough

THE FALLEN TETRALOGY

The Fallen Odyssey: A Parallel Universe Fantasy Novel
The Fallen Aeneid: Book 2 of the Fallen Odyssey
Shadows of the Fallen: Book 3 of the Fallen Odyssey (coming soon)
The Fallen Anabasis: Book 4 of the Fallen Odyssey (coming soon)

ROGUES' GALAXY SERIES

A Knife in the Dark: A Science Fiction Noir Thriller
A Knife in the Dark: Alloyheart
Six Shooter (coming soon)

ABOUT THE AUTHOR

COREY MCCULLOUGH is an independent copy editor, proofreader, ghostwriter, and author. He lives in western Pennsylvania with his amazing wife Vanessa and their two beautiful daughters. His favorite pastimes are reading, writing, playing video games, spending time with his best friend (Vanessa), and, most of all, being a dad.

Instagram @cbenmcc
Facebook.com/mcculloughwrites
Facebook.com/thefallenodyssey
mcculloughauthor@gmail.com
cbmcediting.com

Made in the USA
Middletown, DE
29 October 2021